Napping Princess

The Story of the Unknown Me

KENJI KAMIYAMA

YEN
ON

New York

Napping Princess
The Story of the Unknown Me

KENJI KAMIYAMA

Translation by Yota Okutani

HIRUNEHIME -SHIRANAI WATASHI NO MONOGATARI-
© Kenji Kamiyama/2017"ANCIEN AND THE MAGIC TABLET"Film Partners
First published in Japan in 2017 by KADOKAWA CORPORATION, Tokyo.
English translation rights arranged with KADOKAWA CORPORATION, Tokyo
through TUTTLE-MORI AGENCY, INC., Tokyo.

English translation © 2018 by Yen Press, LLC

Yen On
1290 Avenue of the Americas
New York, NY 10104

Visit us at yenpress.com • facebook.com/yenpress • twitter.com/yenpress • yenpress.tumblr.com • instagram.com/yenpress

First Yen On Edition: June 2018

Yen On is an imprint of Yen Press, LLC.
The Yen On name and logo are trademarks of Yen Press, LLC.

The publisher is not responsible for websites (or their content) that are not owned by the publisher.

Library of Congress Cataloging-in-Publication Data
Names: Kamiyama, Kenji, author, artist. | Okutani, Yota, translator.
Title: Napping princess : the story of the unknown me / Kenji Kamiyama ;
    translation by Yota Okutani.
Other titles: Hirunehime. English
Description: New York, NY : Yen On, June 2018.
Identifiers: LCCN 2018008564 | ISBN 9781975326081 (paperback)
Subjects: | CYAC: Fantasy. | Dreams—Fiction. | Adventure and
    adventurers—Fiction. | BISAC: FICTION / Science Fiction / Adventure.
Classification: LCC PZ7.1.K216 Nap 2018 | DDC [Fic]—dc23
LC record available at https://lccn.loc.gov/2018008564

ISBNs: 978-1-9753-2608-1 (paperback)
        978-1-9753-2613-5 (ebook)

10 9 8 7 6 5 4 3 2 1

LSC-C

Printed in the United States of America

Contents

Chapter 1

Once upon a time, there was a kingdom called Heartland, and all its people were obsessed with machinery.

This kingdom by the sea was covered with mechanical apparatuses and roads, and at its center stood a large castle. The castle doubled as a gigantic factory, and every morning, each citizen would make their way to it by car. The distance from their homes was irrelevant; everybody drove. As such, the kingdom's streets were constantly congested. It took hours to reach the castle, and everybody was constantly late for work. Though the kingdom's skies were always a bright, beautiful blue, the faces of its people were forever clouded with exhaustion.

"The traffic is awful again…," muttered the princess of Heartland, Ancien to Heart, from a glass tower at the edge of the castle.

Though she was the king's actual daughter, she had been imprisoned in the glass tower for various reasons. The world she could see far below her window consisted of roads upon roads, all densely packed with cars.

"Where are they all going?" a stuffed dog asked Ancien, its cheek glued to the window glass. The creature's name was Joy. Though Ancien's companion was only a plushie, it could move on its own and even speak.

Ancien picked Joy up for a cuddle and answered its question while staring out the window.

"They're coming here—to Heartland Castle. They work around the clock to build machines."

From the glass spire's lofty height, the cars didn't appear to be moving at all. It was as if time had stopped—the picture of tedium. Ancien sighed deeply, then hugged Joy tightly.

She had yet to take notice of the motorcycle gracefully weaving among and ahead of the cars trapped in the heavy traffic.

King Heartland, the head of the castle and Ancien's father, held the utmost confidence in the art of building machines. He believed technology would bring happiness to all of humanity.

That was why King Heartland made his citizens craft machinery, and it was also why he made sure each one drove only the newest model of automobile. However, he was unaware that the surplus of cars was responsible for heavy traffic, nor was he aware that the congestion caused all his people to arrive late to work. Even today, the guards stationed at the gate between the town and the castle were yelling angrily at the citizens, but this would never reach the king's ears.

The people who finally made it to the castle would manufacture automobiles in the factory within its walls. They took shifts on the production line so that work could continue day and night. The ties around the employees' necks may as well have been padlocks.

"Man, we only managed four hours of work today," they remarked as they prepared to return home. Of course, this was because they had been late. But since that had become the norm, they didn't sound disappointed about it.

Equally matter-of-fact, the foreman handed them their wages for the day. "I've deducted the missed time from your pay."

This routine repeated daily, without deviation. Peach, a man clothed in a leather jumpsuit with a bandanna around his head, watched the meaningless exchange out of the corner of his eye.

"You've gotta be kidding me," he said with a sigh.

Peach, who had just completed his first shift at Heartland Castle, headed to his beloved motorcycle waiting in the castle's parking lot. He loved the way it could thread through the static rows of cars. No matter how depressed he might feel, riding it through the town's streets always lifted his spirits. He climbed onto the precious vehicle to head home.

"Hey, you. How long are you going to keep riding that old thing?" the foreman called to him in an unfriendly tone.

Peach widened his eyes at the harsh words. The motorcycle was old, true, but it was the first model the castle had ever produced, the S-193. An antique.

"Trade it in for the new model!" the foreman yelled.

Peach, fresh from the countryside, did not yet understand the kingdom's customs.

"As if," Peach replied without thinking, speaking with a flippant tone he often used long ago as a delinquent.

The foreman ignored Peach's rude language and snatched the pay envelope from his hand.

"I'm docking your pay for breaking the rules!" No sooner had he said it than he took two thousand of the three thousand yen from Peach's pay and hurled the rest back at his face.

"Wha—?" Peach yelped in shock, then picked the now-paper-thin envelope up from the ground.

"Starting this month, you're upgrading, too," the foreman yelled at another man.

The other man's vehicle was a slightly outdated model. "But I really like this car," he protested. "Couldn't I—?"

Before the man could finish asking whether he could keep it, the foreman interrupted.

"The rules do not exist to be ignored."

"Right, of course…"

Peach could only watch as the man gave a melancholy chuckle.

It was a typical day in Eastopolis, Heartland's capital. No matter how heavy the traffic might be, no matter how attached one might be to an older vehicle, it mattered not before the rules of the king. In Heartland, the king's word was all that counted.

Despite his power, King Heartland, too, had one great worry—that his own daughter, Ancien, had been born a magic user.

It was foretold that a magic user would bring great strife to the kingdom. In the motor-centric Heartland, anything supernatural was considered a foreign power. Ancien, who had possessed this ability from birth, was able to channel magic through a special tablet.

When Ancien was three, her father gave her a perfectly ordinary stuffed dog. Once she had named it Joy, she wanted more than to merely play with it; she desired to become friends, so she cast her magic on it. The plushie promptly began to move of its own accord, laugh, and speak.

Then, when she was six, a momentous incident occurred. In front of the entire kingdom, Ancien cast her magic on a sidecar-mounted motorcycle she was fond of and transformed it into a robot, which she named Heart. She was met with a flurry of applause and cheers.

Ancien's magic could automate all the town's machinery. The machines might be able to manufacture more equipment themselves without human intervention. All Ancien wanted was to help the townspeople, who were exhausted from labor and traffic jams, but one man opposed her—Bewan, the king's right-hand man and grand inquisitor. He took the tablet and Heart from the girl.

"Ancien's power is dangerous. No doubt, it will end in this kingdom's ruin."

As a result of Bewan's severe advice, Ancien was imprisoned in the glass tower at the castle's edge.

*   *   *

Even now, captive in the glass stronghold, Ancien's only wish was for the kingdom to become a happier place, where people might live with smiles on their faces. Her distrust toward Bewan and the king, who had deemed her magic to be dangerous without any real explanation or discourse, only grew day by day.

One evening, after witnessing a giant explosion occur outside her window, Ancien decided: She wanted to bring joy to everyone with her magic. She wanted the people of Heartland to smile happily without having to fatigue themselves making cars.

The explosions continued; the town was under attack from a giant demon. The creature—black, faceless, and big as a mountain—was rumored to be a plague that had appeared due to Ancien's presence. Was magic truly a source of strife? Ancien wondered whether it was not the other way around, that magic was a power to rid the world of trouble. Together with Joy, Ancien climbed through the glass tower's skylight and jumped out onto its roof. Freezing air blew atop the high turret. Ancien slid down the round top, then carefully made her daring journey toward the castle's center along the narrow ledge provided by the eaves. The evening winds gusted before the setting sun, making Ancien's hair and skirt dance and sway.

The metal door to a room resembling a giant safe swung slowly open. This place was meant to seal away the magical artifacts Bewan had determined to be dangerous. Ancien knew he hoarded them as though they were treasure. Bewan wanted not to rid the world of magic but to harness it for himself—Ancien's tablet was sure to be here.

As she felt around for the light and turned it on, Joy popped into the room and cried, "Look! The magic tablet!"

Approaching the tablet, Ancien noticed Heart in the corner of her vision. Its engine had apparently been cut, and it didn't so much as twitch. Its large, rounded body had been stuffed into a corner, cold and still.

"All this, just because I cast my magic over you... Poor thing."

Prior to its transformation, Heart had been a sidecar-mounted motorcycle free to roam where it pleased. How cruel, then, that upon gaining its autonomy, it had been thrust into this cramped room, never to know how large the world was! For a moment, Ancien motionlessly took in Heart's sorry condition.

Suddenly, the lights gave way to alarms, and police sirens sounded in the distance.

"I'll be back for you later," Ancien promised. She then leaped out of the room along with Joy.

The soldiers hurried into the castle.

"Could it be?!"

Bewan, now aware of the panic, excused himself from the king's presence and started down the path to the glass tower. The soldiers were converging upon the room where he had sealed the magical artifacts. And if someone was after those artifacts...

What a troublesome princess!

As Bewan approached the glass tower, cursing her all the while, Ancien stood outside its walls. She had to get back inside before Bewan arrived and saw that she wasn't in her room. Ancien reached for the small crack in the wall, hitched her foot into it, and scampered back up toward her empty prison.

The glass tower stood past the end of a metal pillar that jutted out from the castle like a thin arm. Bewan stood at one end of the support and pressed a button on the adjacent wall with practiced ease. The device groaned as it extended to the glass tower to form a walkway.

Ancien leaped gracefully along in the shadow of the gradually lengthening shaft, entered the glass tower, and buried herself in the bed. That instant, the castle and tower were connected, and Bewan strode into her room.

He stared at Ancien, who had turned her back to the entrance and pulled the bedsheets over herself. After a few moments of silence, he clicked his tongue in annoyance and returned to the castle.

*   *   *

"…Safe."

Mumbling drowsily, Kokone awoke and pushed herself upright on her mattress. She felt as though she had just dreamed about diving under her covers in the nick of time. Still half-asleep, she touched the smartphone beside her pillow. Its screen displayed the numbers 7:34.

"Oh no! I'm gonna be late!" Kokone exclaimed.

She scooped up the stuffed dog lying next to her and returned her longtime sleeping companion to its place on top of her desk. She speedily folded her futon and put it away, then changed into her uniform. It was a sunny morning in anticipation of the last summer vacation of Kokone's high school career, which would begin tomorrow.

"The Tokyo Olympics are now only three days away, and the final preparations for opening ceremonies are being made at the New National Stadium. The Summer Olympics have not been held in Japan since—"

The news announcer continued in her pleasant voice. In the summer of 2020, all the news concerned the Tokyo Summer Olympics, and the air was thick with excitement all over Japan. Okayama was no exception, despite its distance from Tokyo.

"I overslept, sorry," Kokone apologized as she descended from the second floor to the first, now properly dressed. She hopped over the automobile parts littering the bottom of the stairwell, wove her way through the engines and other clutter scattered on the floor from the hallway to the entrance, and finally arrived at the kitchen. On the kitchen table sat an unfamiliar plastic bag, and inside were a generous number of tomatoes, too many for Kokone and her father, Momotarou, to consume on their own.

"...Dad? Is this Mr. Miyake's payment for the repairs?" Kokone asked her father, poking her head out from the kitchen into the workshop. He didn't respond.

Morikawa Motors, the small auto repair shop that Momotarou ran by himself, opened and closed whenever its owner pleased. This morning, he had skipped breakfast and set straight to working silently. He loved the time he spent engrossed in his tinkering more than anything. Unfortunately, that precious time had been interrupted by a sudden phone call.

"...Did Chairman Shijima really say that?" Momotarou asked, frowning deeply at his smartphone.

"The chairman expressed that if you will not hand him the tablet, he will bring you to trial, as discussed."

"How can you possibly say that *now*?!"

"This is our final warning."

Momotarou could imagine the caller's face, shamelessly assured of his own righteousness in the matter. Despite his malevolent smiles, until that fateful accident, the caller was convinced this was just.

If only this were a fistfight, Momotarou thought, grinding his teeth.

"I bet you wouldn't eat anything 'til lunch if I didn't cook for you..."

Kokone quickly gave up on calling out to her father and began making breakfast. She poured beaten eggs into a preheated pan and listened to the comforting sound of sizzling as it filled the kitchen.

Kokone had been in charge of cooking in the Morikawa household ever since her grandmother had passed away when Kokone was in middle school. There was no way Momotarou, taciturn and competent solely at working with cars, could do any chores whatsoever, and for Kokone, who had lost her mother soon after birth and never had anyone else to fill the role, household tasks were a fact of life. If she overslept, she would inevitably be late for school.

As she was jerking the frying pan to fold the eggs into the shape of an omelet, she sensed Momotarou enter the kitchen from his workshop.

"Dad! Would you at least put away your mahjong tiles?"

Atop the small *kotatsu* table they used as a dining table, the mahjong tiles were still strewn where Momotarou and his friends had used them the previous evening. Momotarou, tired and in no mood to argue, began putting away the scattered pieces.

"Seventeen new arenas have been built in the Bay Zone adjacent to Tokyo Bay. As such, the city's central area has been named the Heritage Zone, and there are plans to use the Yoyogi National Gymnasium and the Nippon Budokan, which hosted events in the last Tokyo Olympics."

Kokone transferred the omelet to a plate while the television relayed news about the Olympics. To an average high schooler living in the countryside, the Olympics might as well have been occurring in a different world entirely. More important to her was how today's omelet was slightly better cooked than usual, and she inspected it with a hint of pride as she placed a few slices of tomato next to it and headed to the living room, plate in hand.

"Mornin'."

"Mm…"

Kokone laid out breakfast, the table now clear of mahjong tiles. Momotarou took the remote in hand and turned the television off. Without so much as a word of thanks, he reached for the chopsticks next to his plate, and though his lack of manners was nothing new, his mood this particular morning seemed to be worse than normal.

"Have you visited Mom's grave yet?"

"Nope."

Kokone sensed something amiss in Momotarou's distant expression, and she pursed her lips.

"Let's eat."

Kokone re-centered herself and put her hands together, then picked up her chopsticks. She cut a bite-size piece of picture-perfect omelet and put it in her mouth; then, with a hint of melodrama, she exclaimed:

"Yum! That's so good! I've really outdone myself this time!"

"..."

Momotarou didn't respond, so Kokone asked, "Did you know my summer vacation starts tomorrow?"

"Oh? Huh."

"Hey, what do you say we take a trip? It's been a while, hasn't it?"

Momotarou's chopsticks briefly paused, but he popped a cut of tomato into his mouth a moment later.

"We used to go all the time, remember? We'd go driving and camping and do all kinds of stuff."

Momotarou drank his miso soup.

"...Mm, guess I could go without this year. Exams and all, y'know!"

"..."

Even when the topic was as important as his daughter's academics, Momotarou remained pensively silent. She had no idea what he was thinking, but he wasn't likely to talk if she questioned him in this state. Knowing how stubborn her father could be, Kokone abandoned her pursuit and quickly polished off the last of her breakfast. The bus would be here soon.

"Whew, I'm done."

Kokone brought her plate to the kitchen sink, took a cup of tea to the still-silent Momotarou, and headed to the altar room.

Kokone's responsibilities included opening the altar room's curtains to let in the brilliant morning sun. There was a traditional homemade figure on the altar—a horse to guide ancestral spirits home during the August *Obon* festival. Fashioned from a cucumber with okra on top, it seemed more motorcycle than horse. It was Momotarou's style.

Kokone muffled a snigger. "Ain't it a bit early for *Obon*, Dad?"

Maybe he wanted his wife to come back as soon as possible. Kokone took a seat in front of the altar and put her hands together. The portrait on the platform depicted her mother, sporting her ever-bright and confident smile.

Kokone slid open the front door with a rattle.

"See ya!" she called.

As before, Momotarou gave no response. Kokone took her phone from her bag and pulled up her messaging app. "*See you later-. ♪,*" she typed. Her message was immediately marked *Read*, but a response didn't arrive for a while.

"Do you want to go to a university in Tokyo at all?"

He did seem interested in her tests, at least.

"Why so curious all of a sudden? You were so quiet a minute ago."

Kokone, though frustrated, typed her response.

"Yeah, I'm shooting for Tokyo. I'm not you, Dad."

"I see.   I'm going to go visit Mom's grave before you.   Might get home late."

"Huh? What's with you? No more questions about it?"

Though her father was usually the quiet type, today was particularly bad. She had written it off as his typical behavior, but there was something clearly off.

"Are the Momotarous getting together today, too? Do you have enough members to play mahjong?"

The "Momotarous" were Kijita and Sawatari, two men who loved mahjong and had pillaged the Morikawa pantry last evening. They had known Momotarou since high school and were his biking pals, bad influences, close friends, customers of Morikawa Motors, and neighbors. Though they were old enough to be considered adults and had families of their own, they were kids at heart, and Kokone called them the Momotarous from a place of affection and slight exasperation.

Tired of communicating by text, Kokone returned to the workshop and sneaked up behind her father as he typed a response.

"Make sure they pay you like they should today, okay?"

Surprised to hear the voice of his texting partner, Momotarou's stoic mask finally cracked a little.

"Got it?!"

"Y-yeah."

Satisfied that Momotarou's expression had returned to normal, Kokone smiled, spun on her heel, and ran to the bus stop. Momotarou wordlessly watched his daughter leave.

She sure has grown, he thought. *Nearly eighteen years old.*

On her way to the bus stop, Kokone saw Kijita outside his home, fixing up his white motorcycle. His appearance suggested a countryside delinquent who had gotten older without outgrowing the behavior, but he was still a proper policeman. He was an unusual officer who had channeled his passion for motorcycles into joining the unit famous for their white bikes.

Though he had been playing mahjong at Kokone's house just a few hours ago, Kijita showed no sign of fatigue. As might be expected of a former delinquent, his stamina was nothing if not admirable.

"Good morning, Mr. Kijita!" Kokone greeted him as she did every morning.

"Yo, Kokone. I'm surprised you're up."

"You guys are too tough for me. Take care of Dad tonight, 'kay?" With that, Kokone dashed down a flight of stone stairs with the Great Seto Bridge to her left. She ran down a narrow street barely wide enough to walk two abreast. Without neglecting to greet her acquaintances, she maneuvered through spaces between houses, crossing streets and alleyways, all seemingly frozen in time for over a decade. Kokone had lived here as long as she could remember, and she knew this route to be the shortest way to the bus stop, though no smartphone would display it.

"Morning, Mr. Sawatari!" Kokone greeted the other member of the Momotarous as she reached a street on the seaside.

Sawatari owned a small company called Sawatari Boating and often did repairs and maintenance in his line of work. He and the grease monkey Momotarou had plenty of common ground when it came to their respective professions. Including the motorcycling Kijita, the Momotarous were tinkerers through and through.

"Morning, Kokone! Energetic as always!"

"I'm not, but I'll do my best!"

Without breaking her stride, Kokone waved to Sawatari and his fishermen.

"Take care of my old man tonight!" she said as she ran along the shallow curve of the seaside street. The bus station was close by.

Taonura Port Station—Kokone took the bus from this stop every day to get to school. Ordinarily, Kokone was the only one at this station, but today, some people were already there when Kokone arrived. Two young men wearing AR goggles were engaged in a passionate conversation. Though it wasn't uncommon to see people typing on unseen keyboards and scrolling rapidly in front of their faces in the city, it was still an alien sight in this small country town. Kokone slyly glanced at the pair as she tried to catch her breath. She recognized the man closest to her from somewhere; his mouth looked familiar, and he seemed intelligent in a geeky sort of way.

"…Hmm? Hey, are you Morio?" Kokone asked excitedly, pulling the goggles off the young man's face.

"Whaaa—?!" yelled the young man, who was indeed Kokone's childhood friend Morio. He was Sawatari's son and the town genius, currently attending a famous science-focused university in Tokyo. They hadn't had much contact since he had left town, but back when he was nearby, he had mentored her like an older brother, though he was more like a younger brother in terms of emotional maturity. He and Kokone had often played together while the Momotarous were drinking.

"I knew it! It is you, Morio!"

"Ko— Kokone…"

Morio shrank away from Kokone and her undisguised joy at their reunion.

"It's been a while! I guess you're on break already? When'd you get back? Have you gotten taller? Man, you used to be so tiny, and you were always following me around."

As Kokone drilled him like a nosy older relative, Morio swallowed his reply to the comment about his height before straightening his spine a bit.

"…Will you stop calling me by my first name? Geez…," he said, his cheeks reddening in embarrassment.

Kokone didn't notice this and, grinning, slung her arms around Morio's shoulders.

"Aw, really? But it'd be so weird to call you 'my bro Morio' or 'Mr. Morio.'"

Morio's friend, who had been watching their conversation, whispered into Morio's ear:

"Hey, she's Gruff's daughter, right? You know each other?"

Morio cocked his head at the unfamiliar name Gruff. His friend, seemingly annoyed, gave another hint. "You know, the one from the auto shop at the top of the hill…"

"Oh, Gruff Track."

Morio recalled the sight of Momotarou's back, one he had become well accustomed to in childhood. A jersey tracksuit, emblazoned with a skull and wings of gold and black on the back. A design like that was rarely seen in these parts, but it was consistent with Momotarou's past as a delinquent.

"I hear that's what the kids call him nowadays," Kokone interjected, unbothered by her father's unflattering nickname. Though he swore like a sailor, his temper was short, and his expression was always somewhat unpleasant, Kokone knew that his straightforwardness and quality of work were well respected. She was proud of her father's dedication to his craft, although it would be hard to admit it to his face.

Kokone's one-sided questioning showed no signs of ceasing even after they boarded the bus.

"Hey, Morio, what school do you go to? I wanna go to Tokyo for school, too."

Morio cocked an eyebrow at this, but before he could say a word, his friend interrupted. "You wouldn't make it there even if you tried for the rest of your life."

"Seriously?! It's that far…? Well, maybe I can get there if I take a plane…"

Kokone had completely missed the point. Morio and his friend looked at each other.

Though Kokone aspired to go to Tokyo, she had no practical knowledge of the place. Her life in the country—meddling in her father's business, joining the Momotarous for the occasional mahjong session, and chatting about nothing at all at school—was extremely comfortable. Kokone, already in her third year of high school, was innocent and carefree, to put it kindly—actually, to put it unkindly, she still had the immaturity of a child who couldn't see beyond her immediate surroundings.

"You managed to put that on my pickup?" the old man asked Momotarou. He had popped by Morikawa Motors to check on his truck, which had a punctured tire, while he was out for a walk with his dog.

"Yeah, somehow," replied Momotarou, who happened to be working on the truck just then. He looked up at the device attached to the top of the truck, which resembled a rounded security camera, with a hint of pride.

After seating the old man in the passenger seat and the dog in the driver's seat, Momotarou leaned in from the driver's side and began explaining how to operate the camera-equipped satnav. Momotarou connected his cracked tablet to the gadget and swiftly brought up the control menu.

"Tap this and where you're goin', and the map'll come up," Momotarou explained while tapping the screen. The old man and his dog followed carefully along.

"After that, press this again."

The old man sighed, impressed, and happily commented, "I'm real grateful to ya for doing all this for me, but you can't be making much if old geezers like me are your only clientele."

"Huh? Nah, that ain't true." Momotarou looked away and continued: "The older they are, the more cash they've got."

Of course, the old man was aware that Momotarou didn't mean this and that it was his way of drawing attention away from his embarrassment. Momotarou remembered how the seniors who came to him had been complaining that driving was becoming increasingly difficult, and so, when they visited him for repairs, he would ask them whether they wanted an extra something and then dispassionately attach the "magic gizmo" to their cars. Momotarou never expressed his kindness directly, but the old man gave him a wrinkly smile, any-way, recognizing the generosity.

"I wonder. Anyway, how much?" he asked.

"Hmm? Just the repairs for the tire. Two thousand yen."

Generous as always. The old man handed Momotarou the two thousand yen, along with a plastic bag containing a watermelon.

"In that case, take this."

Momotarou took the watermelon with no protest, a ghost of a smile on his face. The old man climbed into the driver's seat with an "Alley-oop."

"All right, to Koyama Hospital," he said to the tablet. The device immediately displayed the hospital's location on a map, so the old man tapped the screen as Momotarou had instructed. When he saw the screen loading, Momotarou shut the vehicle's door and backed away a step. The car began quietly pulling away, then suddenly halted. Confused, the driver peered around the corner just as another car zoomed through the street in front of the small truck.

Momotarou had installed an autobrake system, which predicted the trajectories of other cars and stopped the truck as needed to avoid accidents. Once the other car had passed, the old man's truck moved forward again, and the steering wheel turned to the right even though he wasn't touching it.

Momotarou had been watching the spectacle with some satisfaction and called after the old man, "Hey, geezer! Keep your hands on the wheel! I'll get in trouble if ya don't!"

Self-driving cars were not yet available to the public. The automobile-industry giant Shijima Motors was to release this revolutionary technology to the world at the Olympic tournament in three days—the athletes were to ride in self-driving cars. Only subsequently would the technology become publicly available. Or at least that was the plan.

"I hear ya," the old man replied, unaware of how revolutionary the technology in front of him was.

"...Geez, I swear." Momotarou sighed. His expression, though, was cheerful.

He returned to his workshop and gazed lovingly at a photo on the wall of a younger, smiling Momotarou, his arms wrapped around the shoulders of Kokone's mother, Ikumi.

* * *

Recently, the kingdom had suffered periodic attacks from a giant demon. These attacks were said to be a disaster brought about by Ancien's birth.

Tonight, the pitch-black sea swelled up like a mountain once again, and the demon appeared amid a spray of seawater. Its face had no nose or eyes, its only feature a gaping mouth like a portal to hell. Its inhumanly long limbs created waves, capsizing ships, and it made a beeline for the Gulf Area, which was in the thick of rush hour. The people, trapped in their cars without any hope of escaping forward or backward, gazed up at the demon as it stepped over the congested roads. The demon began popping the cars into its mouth, one by one, like a child with pieces of candy. Explosions rang through the kingdom of Heartland.

Though Bewan had advised the ruler of Heartland to banish the princess from the kingdom, the king could not bear to do such a thing to his beloved daughter. Instead, the king had doubled down on his faith in machinery and placed the kingdom's fate in its mechanical hands, constructing giant machines called Engine Heads that were designed to defeat the demon. Upon receiving news that the monster had appeared in the Gulf Area, the king leaped into action.

"Machine Military Division, activate the Engine Heads!" he ordered into his amplifier.

Receiving this command, Engine Heads immediately sprang to life...or they would have, if it had been possible. Multiple pilots worked in an Engine Head at a time—one captain to serve as the brain, a director in each limb to relay the captain's orders, three steersmen in each limb to move the limbs according to the orders relayed by the directors, and a great many other soldiers assigned to various other body parts—all working together to make a single step possible.

Upon receiving the king's orders, the captain bellowed into the microphone connecting him to the rest of the body, loud enough to damage his throat:

"Left leg! Step forward twenty yards at an angle of seven degrees!"

The left leg's director, not missing a word of the captain's orders, respectfully saluted the captain and sharply turned toward his three steersmen, who were seated in what resembled exercise bikes. The director repeated loudly:

"Forward, twenty yards, seven degrees!"

The steersmen simultaneously pushed down on their weighty pedals. The culmination of Heartland's technology was also the culmination of their traditions and inefficiency.

"Forward, twenty yards, seven degrees!" No matter what, they were obligated to repeat their orders. Their pedaling quickened as they huffed and puffed. Once the numbers on the console displayed maximum speed, the three leaned back with their body weights in sync and angled the cockpit backward.

The Engine Heads' hangar door opened, and the pilots readied themselves for their foray. Three Engine Heads, their round metal bodies attached to long ladderlike limbs, took their first steps into the night. Treading carefully so as to avoid the town's congested streets, they made their way toward the demon, each footfall resounding like an earthquake.

The demon was sitting now, and the vehicles it had carelessly picked up were spewing fire that set the surrounding area alight. The people had long since abandoned their cars. Unfazed by the black smoke billowing into the sky, the demon continued tossing them into its mouth. Suddenly, as if it had realized something, the demon stopped.

* * *

From his room's window, Bewan watched the demon's flickering silhouette against the burning town and flames.

"Hmph…," he snickered, then he walked to his desk and took a seat. On the desk were many vials and beakers of ominously colored liquids, along with a variety of books and texts, all neatly ordered. At the desk's center was a typewriter of odd design, connected to a glass tube. Bewan gave a sinister chuckle and typed at the device, *clack, clack*, and neon-green smoke spiraled through the glass tube. Bewan pressed the final key with another loud *clack*. The green plume arced, forced its way through the glass tube's lid, and spilled out. The words Bewan had just typed floated into view inside the cloud of smoke, then transformed into a crow and took to the sky toward the demon at a blistering speed.

Every time this menace appeared, Bewan secretly and masterfully cast a spell that increased the demon's power. Bewan looked through the window with a grin, eager to see how effective today's spell would be. He dreamed of the day that he might expose the king as incompetent, drive him out, and take the throne for himself. To that end, Bewan daily researched ways to make the most of this demon.

"Those won't do. Only a robot powered by magic can defeat that demon…," muttered Ancien dejectedly. The glass tower offered a fantastic view of the town. Even so, all she could do was to watch as the Engine Heads slowly approached the monster.

The demon, who had taken notice of the machines, kept its center of gravity low and tackled the foremost Engine Head. The creature's movements were incomparably elegant in contrast to its slow and clumsy mechanical foe, which was easily taken off-balance.

"Right leg, backward twenty-five yards, twenty degrees!" ordered the captain in a panic, but the steersmen could not pedal quickly enough. The tackled Engine Head fell to the ground without a chance of retaliation. The king of Heartland watched on, not bothering to hide his frustration.

Heartland's citizens observed the losing battle from below; nearby, Peach, sporting a jacket emblazoned with a winged skull, aimed an oversize gun at the demon. He aligned his sights and fired. The bullet hit the monster right in its back, but as it turned in Peach's direction, it appeared to be unharmed.

Peach waved his arms at the demon as if to tell it who had fired. Once the demon had taken notice of him and made a move to capture him, Peach leaped onto his motorcycle and rode away. The demon chased him, long arm outstretched, but it could not catch up to the young man weaving effortlessly through the congested streets. Ancien saw the demon chasing the small form from her tower.

"...Who is that?!"

Ancien hurriedly adjusted the magnification on her binoculars and took a closer look at the man who had single-handedly changed the battle's course. She couldn't make out his face with his back toward the castle, but she clearly saw his leather jacket and the winged skull on it.

"A pirate?!"

Peach was obviously on a motorcycle and not a ship, but the emblem billowing in the wind was much like a pirate's flag. To Ancien, who knew of pirates only from ancient texts, Peach could be nothing else. Though she had not even seen his face, Ancien sensed great potential in him.

"Joy, let's defeat the demon using that man as bait!"

Joy saluted Ancien with a buccaneer-style "Aye, aye, sir!"

The two left the glass tower for the room where the magical artifacts were sealed. Joy, with surprising speed and strength, knocked out the guards, and the two opened the heavy door just wide enough to slip through. This time, they would recover Heart and the magic tablet.

*   *   *

Ancien took the newly reactivated Heart by the hand and led it outside. Though it stood on two legs, it still resembled its original form as a motorcycle and sidecar in its round body.

"Let's go, Heart! Come with me!"

Heart took a few steps—*glank, glank*—then looked up at Ancien inquisitively, head cocked.

"I'll cast Spirit on you this time!" she said.

Spirit was said to be this world's ultimate magic, capable of even granting people powers of flight.

Ancien entered the spell into the tablet, turned it toward Heart, and hit the ENTER button. Heart transformed back into a sidecar-mounted motorcycle. Ancien hopped onto the motorcycle, and Joy into the sidecar.

Joy pumped a fist into the air and gave a shout to kick off the journey. Ancien pulled the accelerator all the way back, and Heart's tires spun to life and accelerated with a bang.

Peach, riding along the road to the abandoned Gulf Area, glanced behind him. The demon was still in pursuit. He exhaled a sigh of relief, glad to have successfully drawn it away from the castle. He faced forward, only to see that somebody had abandoned a car on the road in front of him.

"!"

Peach turned his handlebars sharply to avoid a crash, but he was thrown from his motorcycle. As the monster approached, he looked around and saw that his gun had, fortunately, fallen close by. He leaped for it, using the momentum to carry himself to his feet and run toward his foe in one smooth motion. The demon lowered its stance and reached for Peach with its right hand. Peach fired at it and blew its middle finger off. He could see the automobiles that the demon had swallowed in the wound. Was the beast composed of the cars…? If so, his gun probably wouldn't be able to inflict a fatal wound. The demon's finger fell next to the rattled Peach, and cars tumbled from the severed digit with an incredible racket.

The wound began healing itself rapidly. Apparently, the demon had regenerative abilities. Peach discarded his useless gun. At this rate, he would be killed. Was there nothing to be done?

At that moment, he heard the familiar sound of a motorcycle engine nearing. As he faced the quickly approaching roar, he thought he might be dreaming. The sidecar-mounted motorcycle coming in his direction was an S-193, and if that weren't enough, its riders were a small girl and a plushie!

Ancien parked Heart in front of the flabbergasted young man and jumped off the motorcycle. She then rounded Peach and took a close look at the mark on his back.

"I knew it—you're a pirate!"

Clueless, Peach forgot about the demon for an instant and took another look at Ancien. Ancien had put on a straw hat, the sort she imagined pirates might wear, and a jacket with a skull on its back. This girl, who had appeared in the direst of circumstances, seemed to be enjoying herself.

"All right! You're part of my crew now. All aboard!"

Ancien leaped back onto Heart and revved up the engine. The noise brought Peach back to his senses, and he grabbed on to the moving sidecar and vaulted into it. Immediately after, the demon's hand slammed into the ground where he had just been.

As the earth rumbled and quaked, and the road peeled up in a cloud of dirt, Heart sped away as quickly as it could amid the hail of asphalt fragments before the haze could settle. The demon, having lost sight of the source of its irritation, had no choice but to give up.

"What's your name?" Ancien asked the "pirate." They'd been driving for a while since their escape.

"...Peach," he muttered. He had been watching the road behind them until now, and he turned to Ancien for the first time since they had gotten on the motorcycle.

"Peach, huh?" Ancien smiled. She repeated his name over and over in her heart.

* * *

"Isn't Peach a princess's name…?"

Kokone mumbled to herself facedown on her classroom desk. She savored the fading remnants of her sweet dream. "…It's been a while since I've dreamed about that…"

"Oh, you were dreaming, were you, Morikawa?"

Kokone would have fallen back asleep but for the voice of her exasperated teacher.

"It isn't summer vacation yet!"

Kokone lifted herself from her desk. "Hee-hee, whoops." She smiled bashfully and played it off as a joke.

The class exploded with laughter. The teacher sighed, slapped Kokone lightly on the head with the attendance folder, and slowly returned to his desk, smiling.

"This summer vacation is a truly crucial time in your lives. Everyone, make the most of it," he said. Noticing that Kokone was once again losing focus, he added, more firmly, "Be sure not to sleep through it. Got it, Morikawa?"

Kokone's friend Chiko shook her awake from the seat behind hers. Kokone forced her body upright and raised her hand.

"Yup! I'm listening. Definitely."

"All right, come back nice and rested next semester, you hear?"

As if on cue, the students stood, their desks and chairs rattling against the floor. Their final summer vacation of high school had just started. The students bowed to their teacher, their expressions radiant.

Chapter 2

"I'm gonna go visit Mom's grave."

After he let Kokone know, Momotarou began prepping to go out. He couldn't rest until he had taken care of the morning's phone call. His plan was to first go see his late spouse and then go to Tokyo.

After changing from his trademark tracksuit into an unfamiliar formal suit, albeit necktie-less and collar popped, he transferred his phone, keys, and wallet to his pockets. He cut a few of the roses from the windowsill to decorate the grave. Roses had been his wife's favorite flower. Then he had one more task: He had to retrieve something from Kokone's room, which he would ordinarily not step foot in at all. He didn't need to search long; he found what he was looking for in front of Kokone's cork bulletin board full of pictures—the plush dog, Joy.

Joy was a plushie that Ikumi had held dear since her own childhood and a precious treasure to Kokone, who had no memories of her mother.

"Kokone's taken good care of it," Momotarou muttered.

He examined the pictures of a young Kokone, and taken aback by how quickly she had grown up, he picked Joy up and sat in the desk's chair for a man-to-man talk.

"…You're the only one who knows everything that happened."

Momotarou sighed heavily and turned the toy over. There was a zipper on its back, and the compartment could contain one small object. Momotarou opened the zipper and forced his cracked tablet, the one that converted normal cars into self-driving ones, into the compartment. He then tucked the deformed plushie under his arm and left the house.

Ikumi's resting place was atop a hill with a view of the Great Seto Bridge and the ocean. Under the blue summer sky, Momotarou placed the flowers, incense, and the plushie containing the tablet beside the gravestone. He stood in front of her resting place, a serene expression on his face.

"Got another call from your father's company this morning. They say they'll sue if I don't hand the tablet over to him." Slowly, Momotarou explained to Ikumi what had happened on the phone that morning. "…And as for custody of Kokone, well, they can forget about that." He ground his teeth.

They had been the ones who told him and Ikumi never to contact them after the couple had announced their marriage. They hadn't known of Kokone's birth, nor had they attended Ikumi's funeral—so why care now?

"…But I think we need to talk once, face-to-face. So I'm off to Tokyo."

Momotarou, imagining that Ikumi might tell him no, that it would be fruitless, placed his hand on her gravestone. The ocean breeze blew against the smoke billowing up from the lit incense, and the smoke wavered.

"It's all right. I was hopin' to talk to your old man at some point." Momotarou took his hand from the gravestone and reached for his bag. At that moment, he felt somebody's presence and straightened himself to see who it was. A uniformed police officer stood in front of him.

"Hmm…?"

As a former delinquent, Momotarou's relationship with the law was historically not the best, but he couldn't imagine why a policeman might be glaring at him as he stood by his wife's grave. Another uniformed policeman and two plainclothesmen joined the first officer to approach Momotarou and stand behind him.

"You're Momotarou Morikawa?" the oldest one asked. Based on his standard accent, it seemed he wasn't from around here. He withdrew a small notebook from his pocket, and Momotarou, seeing it, more or less grasped the situation.

"They called the cops before I even left for Tokyo…"

"You're accused of breaking into Shijima Motors' system and stealing data. We've taken the liberty of searching your house as well, seeing how it's an urgent matter."

Momotarou felt his blood boiling, but he was no longer the delinquent he had once been. He jammed his fist into his pocket and looked at Joy. Softly—too softly for anyone else to hear—he whispered:

"Joy, it's up to you…"

"…I need to see Mr. Shijima."

From inside a large sedan some distance away, a man watched the officers put Momotarou in the police car. The man, sitting in the back of the sedan, held a smartphone displaying his call history, which included yesterday's call to Momotarou. His face, with its bold features and black beard, looked exactly like Grand Inquisitor Bewan's from Kokone's dream.

"When you sleep, you're out like a light, huh, Kokone?" commented Chiko while cleaning the school grounds with a bamboo broomstick.

"Huh? What's that mean?"

Chiko had intended to poke a little fun at the ever-napping Kokone with an old maxim, but she had nothing to say in the face of absent-mindedness unbefitting a third-year in high school.

Kokone was oblivious to her friend's silence, too, and continued, "I was hanging out with my dad's friends last night, almost 'til dawn."

Kokone mimed the placement of mahjong tiles.

Chiko, past the point of exasperation, raised her voice in distress. "Are you okay?!"

"Yup!" Kokone produced a ten-thousand-yen bill from her pocket and proudly showed it to Chiko. "And I got paid."

Chiko started to argue that she was more worried about Kokone's health, but Kokone interrupted.

"But I'm always sleepy even when I'm not up late… Is that a skill?"

"Of course it's not," Chiko replied, and the two burst out laughing. They resumed sweeping.

"Come to think of it, where are you going to study this summer?" Chiko asked.

"Hmm. Might be tough, since we don't have a lot of money. I sort of asked this morning, but my dad didn't reply…"

Smiling, Kokone casually explained her unfortunate situation. Chiko stopped her sweeping.

"Probably got paid in groceries today, too… Wish he'd stop being so generous already… He's still modding cars, you know," Kokone complained, still sweeping.

"You don't talk at home?"

"Nope." She threw her hands up in the air. "These days, he'll even text 'Let's eat' if I let him…"

"Seriously…?"

Though Kokone appeared untroubled about it at first glance, her sweeping came to a stop.

Two male classmates suddenly burst between the conversing Kokone and Chiko. The boys used their momentum to climb over the rear gate, raising a hand in apology after they landed on the other side. They were planning to skip out on chores.

"Them again…" Kokone picked up a small stone from underfoot and, with perfect baseball pitcher form, threw it at the pair. "Come back here!"

Accuracy would be difficult from where she stood far away, but the stone hit one of the two in the head. The boy, more out of combined astonishment and embarrassment than pain, dropped to the ground.

Kokone, the daughter of a former delinquent, was athletically gifted and had a strange sense of justice—she wouldn't stand for fraud or deceit. She put a fist up and claimed her victory, then lowered her voice.

"And it's the last summer vacation of high school, too. What am I going to do…?"

The athletic club's shouts and the brass band's music sounded in the distance.

After the two girls finished cleaning, they headed to the hallway sink to wash their hands.

"Are you gonna visit your relatives?" Chiko asked Kokone, twisting the faucet.

"I live at home, and I don't have any other relatives."

"But your mom lives in Germany, doesn't she?"

"Huh? What do you mean?"

"What do *you* mean?" Chiko furrowed her brow at Kokone's confusion. "For an essay in middle school, didn't you write that your mom lives in Germany?"

"Oh, that. Geez, your memory is really something… That was a lie!"

"Wha—?!"

Chiko nearly dropped the handkerchief she was wiping her hands with.

Kokone laughed. "I got tired of people asking 'Why isn't your mother around?' and 'Why don't you know what your name means?' and 'If the characters for your name mean "heart" and "wing," shouldn't your name be read "Kokoha" instead of "Kokone"?' so I just lied."

For a moment, Chiko began doubting the very foundation of her friendship with Kokone, who had, by her own very blunt admission, been lying to her for six years. Then she realized that only Kokone would write such an unapologetic lie in an essay to retaliate against a form of bullying, and she couldn't help but smile.

"…You're a real idiot, Kokone, but I think it's cute."

Kokone found comfort in the warm praise from her close friend. "Thanks, buddy!"

Elated, she threw herself at Chiko, and Chiko caught her in an embrace. Having known her for so long, Chiko knew that Kokone's carefree laughter often veiled her insecurity, and that fact crossed her mind as Kokone's soft, naturally reddish hair touched her nose.

"Hey, Morikawa!"

As the two shared an emotional embrace in the hallway, the teacher's panicked shout hit them like a splash of cold water. Though he was always telling people not to run in the halls, he dashed toward them. "I just got a call! Your father was arrested by the police!"

Kokone's face paled at the revelation.

The distance between school and Kojima Police Station wasn't short by any means, but Kokone didn't have time to wait for the bus. She ran down the road by the harbor with all the speed she could muster and burst into the police station without so much as stopping to catch her breath.

"Hey, Kokone!" Kijita, one of the Momotarous, had rushed to the scene. Though he was a police officer, he was off duty today and had come wearing sandals and a replica of the tracksuit Bruce Lee had sported in *The Game of Death*.

The moment she saw Kijita, she first thought of her father's modded vehicles—the alterations must have become an issue, for some reason or another, and he'd been arrested.

But the situation was far more complex than that.

"I was surprised, too, so I asked around, but apparently, the investigation is classified. They won't tell me where they've taken him."

Kokone's expression stiffened at the phrase *the investigation is classified.*

What did Dad do?

Kijita told her he would come visit her once he had figured out what was going on. Kokone relented and reluctantly went home.

Before Kokone knew it, her feet were carrying her to Ikumi's grave. Part of the reason was because Momotarou had been arrested while he was visiting the grave, but she was also confused—what was happening? What should she do?

Kokone arrived at the grave with vague intentions of searching for clues, though she knew she couldn't expect to find anything concrete. She saw Joy sitting in front of the flowers that Momotarou had offered to the grave, and she crouched down.

"Why is Joy here?"

Water still clung to the rose petals, and the incense had recently burned out. Kokone reasoned that Momotarou had not completed his visit before being arrested. Why had he brought the plushie here? She began brainstorming.

She lifted Joy and saw that the toy's exterior was slightly deformed. It looked like something rectangular had been placed inside. Kokone unzipped Joy's back and extracted the object.

She'd seen it before—a cracked tablet Momotarou used in his work. Wondering why it was here, Kokone put it back inside Joy, and as the waters around the Seto Inland Sea glittered in the sunset at her back, she hurried back.

*   *   *

"I'm home."

Kokone opened the perpetually unlocked front door, kicked off her white dirt-stained slip-ons, and stepped inside.

She sensed that something was off. "Is somebody here?" she murmured. The house was typically littered with car engine parts and the like, but the clutter wasn't in the same place as usual. With Joy in one hand, Kokone tensed in the now-silent corridor of her home.

Kokone took off her sweaty shirt in the washroom and grabbed a polo shirt meant for club activities. She slipped her arms through the sleeves as she walked and tried to calm her breathing, but she was hit with a sudden wave of fatigue, so she lay down on the tatami floor of the altar room.

"Where did they take Dad...?" muttered Kokone. Using the tablet-stuffed Joy as a pillow, she rolled onto her back. Motionless, she stared at the photo of Ikumi on the lintel. Unlike Momotarou's parents in the picture next to it, she looked so young; one would never guess she was deceased already. It was hard to believe such a radiant smile belonged to somebody no longer on this earth. She was already gone by the time Kokone was old enough to understand the world around her, so all she knew about her mother was that she had gone back to work mere days after having Kokone and passed shortly after, and that she was beautiful.

"Hey, Mom. What do you think Dad did?" Kokone asked her mother's photo in the silent altar room. Coming to her senses, Kokone turned over, sat up, and shared her real feelings with her mother.

"...Y'know, Mom, I don't know anything about you. You died in an accident just after I was born... Dad wouldn't tell me anything more about you..."

Kokone rarely spoke to her mother, but she realized several things in doing so now.

Having no memories of her mother was one thing, but Momotarou had never told her a single story to fill in the gaps, abnormally silent about her. Ever since she was a small child, she had realized his behavior was a choice rather than just part of his personality, but at some point, she had stopped asking about her mother and become content to think of her as a beautiful woman in a photograph. She still thought little more of her mother than that. She was, in short, a rather ungrateful daughter.

"…What were you like when you were my age?" Kokone asked her mother's portrait. She couldn't stop herself from asking, even though she knew she would receive no reply. Normally, her mother was the last thing on her mind, and this may have been the first time she wanted to have a conversation so badly.

"…Did you go to college?"

The sinking sun's rays peeked through the gaps in the curtains, and Kokone was drawn back to reality.

"…Argh, what am I supposed to do…?"

Kokone's body went limp. Her exhaustion from last night's mahjong and her father's arrest overwhelmed her, and her eyelids became too heavy for her to keep open. Barely conscious, Kokone hugged Joy tightly.

"Do something, Mom…," she mumbled weakly before her eyes drooped shut.

*   *   *

Below the great bridge arching above the calm sea stood a harbor town, long forgotten by man. The town was called Hill Mountain, and its main industry was fishing. At the edge of the settlement was a sea cliff, eroded by the waves. Nearby stood a lighthouse, its purpose fulfilled long ago, slightly crooked and alone.

As a pleasant southern breeze blew past the lighthouse and rippled through the grass growing from the dirt atop the mineral deposits, a lone young man was returning with a cornucopia of food. Since the last demon attack, Peach had chosen to work with Ancien.

Deciding to shield the unworldly princess from her pursuers, he had returned to his hometown to help her hide. He had renovated the lighthouse's basement, which he had discovered as a child, into Ancien's hideout.

Peach opened the lighthouse's door, which was just large enough for one person to squeeze through. Hidden nearby were stairs connecting the ground level to the basement. He descended, making sure nobody was watching.

In the basement, Ancien, the tablet opposite her, was attempting to draw up a spell to invoke the magic called Spirit.

"Did it work this time?"

The hideout's walls were plastered white, much like a Mediterranean home, and the interior was very pleasant. Though the entrance was underground, the hideout's rear had a view of the cape and the ocean. Joy sat on a windowsill carved out of the stone and looked out with glee.

"Man, Joy could talk right away," she grumbled to herself.

"Heh, I'm special!" boasted Joy with a puffed-out chest.

At that moment, the two heard something close by and simultaneously shared a glance.

"Peach is home!"

Joy ran toward the entrance, and Ancien, clutching the precious tablet to her chest, wasn't far behind.

"Welcome home, Peach!"

The hideout's lower floor was a garage, open on one side to offer a view of the sea and its great bridge.

Heart sat at the edge of the garage, perfectly still, unable to move on its own. Peach stood in front of the machine with a complicated expression on his face as Ancien and Joy approached, but his eyes softened when he noticed them.

"How's it going? Have you finished writing the ultimate spell to bring machines to life?"

"Not yet... I'm hoping it works this time," Ancien replied. She glanced uncertainly at her tablet.

Peach laughed heartily to raise Ancien's spirits.

"It'll be all right. Just give it a go!"

"...Okay!"

Ancien took a firmer grasp of her tablet with a determined look and began reciting the spell she had just finished writing. Joy proudly looked up at Ancien.

"With spirit alone, we can soar. Heart, come to consciousness and grasp freedom in your hands!"

Ancien confidently touched her index finger to the tablet and raised her voice. "Enter!"

The spell flew off into the distance with a *shwoo*.

Ancien, Peach, and Joy stared at Heart in the silent garage and swallowed.

"...Oh!" Peach broke the silence with a cry of surprise. He had noticed the light on Heart's chest blinking.

"Yes!" Ancien exclaimed.

Just as Joy leaped up in triumph, something happened.

Heavy footsteps approached the trio as two handgun-wielding soldiers walked into the garage.

The three froze at the sight of the barrels pointed at them. Then, from behind the soldiers, appeared Grand Inquisitor Bewan.

"I've finally found you, Princess!"

But we were so careful... Peach gritted his teeth in frustration and stepped between Ancien and Bewan, glaring at the latter.

"You will be returning to the glass tower for the crime of using magic."

"Are those really the king's orders?!" Though Peach had never met the king, he couldn't imagine a man would do that to his own daughter, ruler of a nation or not.

Bewan snorted at Peach's protest. "What a silly question… However, if you kindly hand me that tablet, I will ensure that the king grants you mercy." He offered his condescending proposal with a devilish smile.

* * *

Ding-dong—Kokone awoke to the sound of the doorbell.

The room was pitch-black, and Kokone realized she had been sleeping for some time.

…*Dad?* Kokone thought sleepily.

The doorbell rang once more. Kokone hurried to her feet and went to see who it was on the security monitor in the hallway. On the screen was a bearded man in an expensive-looking suit. She had never seen him before, and yet she recognized him from somewhere.

"He's…!"

The man was the spitting image of Bewan from her dream. She took a closer look at the monitor, trying to get ahold of her confused thoughts. Unaware that Kokone was watching, the man leaned toward the camera as if peering in.

"She should be home by now. I'm taking the daughter with me… We can't have the Tokyo police taking her into custody with her guardian absent," he said to the two men dressed in black behind him as he checked his expensive-looking watch. She could hear him through the intercom's microphone.

"Tokyo police…?" This had to have something to do with her

father's arrest. Though she realized this immediately, a wave of panic and fear washed over her, leaving her paralyzed.

At that moment, her phone's messaging app chirped from her skirt's pocket. Kokone pulled it out in a hurry and checked the screen.

"Dad?!"

The message was from her missing father.

"*If this man shows up, he's a bad guy*," the message read.

A picture was attached to the exceedingly blunt message. It depicted a young Momotarou and Ikumi, who was holding Joy. Behind them stood a man with a fake-looking smile, his upper head cut off by the edge of the photo… It was the bearded man on the intercom.

"It's… It's him!"

Watanabe, the man who looked exactly like Grand Inquisitor Bewan, set his hand on Kokone's front door and gently attempted to slide it open. It did so without any resistance.

"This lack of security will be the death of these country yokels," he muttered to himself.

Watanabe gestured to the two behind him and walked into the house uninvited. He scanned the dark interior.

"Not home yet… Good-for-nothing girl."

Unaware that Kokone was holding her breath in the living room just one sliding screen away, he ordered his underlings, "We need that tablet. It wasn't in the evidence the police gathered. Find it at all costs!"

The men split up to search the second floor and the kitchen, and Watanabe headed for the living room. Kokone sneaked away to the altar room next door.

"It's dark…" Without any reservation, Watanabe tugged the cord attached to the living room light.

Kokone, now in the altar room, held her breath. Where could she hide?

"Mr. Watanabe! I think I found it!"

"Hmm?" When one of his men called to him from the kitchen, Watanabe left the living room for later. Kokone, breathing shallowly, strained to hear their conversation.

"You idiot! That's a whiteboard!"

"…Sorry."

Kokone heard a slap to the underling's head. Watanabe now seemed to be searching the kitchen himself. No doubt he would return soon. Kokone started to slip out of the altar room while she could, but just then, the phone in her hand rang, briefly but audibly.

"?!"

Kokone could sense that Watanabe and his underling had noticed. Despite her fear, she managed to take a look.

"*I left the tablet at the grave. Don't let them have it*," read the message from Momotarou.

"…You shoulda told me earlier!" Kokone replied to the untimely text before she could stop herself.

She took a peek at Joy on the floor of the altar room. Kokone was still behind the sliding door, hidden from the intruders, but she would be visible if she moved now.

"Damn it!"

He had definitely heard a cell phone and a girl's voice. Confident, Watanabe quietly made his way back to the living room—but nobody was there. His eye was drawn to the plushie lying on the floor of the altar room. He had seen the old stuffed dog before.

"This plushie…?!"

Watanabe picked it up. Unlike its soft head, its body was somewhat harder. There was clearly something inside. Watanabe found the zipper on the plushie's back and opened it. Soon after, he gave a triumphant cry.

"…It's here! Hey, I found it!!"

But no matter how much he pulled, the tablet wouldn't come out. Joy's body simply stretched with every tug, amazingly without tearing.

"Joy…!" Kokone had been watching from between the two sliding doors of her hiding place. She immediately regretted her careless outburst. "What am I doing?"

She buried herself between two mattresses, desperate not to make another sound. She felt her phone drop from her pocket in the process, but right now, that was the least of her concerns.

Watanabe glared at the closet. "Hiding there, were you?"

He walked up and opened its doors, but all he saw were a bunch of mattresses and a smartphone with a case clearly belonging to a high school girl. Watanabe picked up the phone. Its messaging app was still open, and its screen displayed a photo of Watanabe with the message *"If this man shows up, he's a bad guy"* underneath.

"…'A bad guy,' huh?"

Candid as always, Momotarou Morikawa.

Momotarou had always looked everyone in the eye, including Watanabe, and spoken his mind. Momotarou wasn't even properly educated and got results by convincing people through his intuitiveness and actions. He was the type of person Watanabe hated most. The thought of Momotarou helplessly detained in an interrogation room, being questioned ceaselessly by the police, was enough to bring a smile to his face. But despite that, Momotarou had managed to contact his daughter using his phone.

Damn it. But soon there'll be no more of that.

Watanabe's underling had returned from the second floor while he'd been following this train of thought. Watanabe put his hand to the other sliding door, all but declaring checkmate. But then...

"Kokone, you home?"

"!"

A blithe-sounding young man called from the kitchen entrance. Watanabe had never heard the voice before.

"My old man heard your dad got arrested. Said to come by, make sure you're okay... My old man and Mr. Kijita will be over later."

The voice belonged to Morio, Kokone's childhood friend who had come home to Shimotsui from Tokyo that morning. He had come to check up on Kokone, holding a bag with a cheap Origin-brand bento box.

Though Watanabe hadn't been able to capture the girl, he did have the tablet.

Aware that the young man was going to come in without waiting for a reply, Watanabe and his men left from the back porch. They had taken their shoes off at the entrance, so the three could feel the mud seeping into their socks. This was ridiculous. As a sadistic rage welled up within him, Watanabe considered taking it out on one of his underlings.

"Contact Takamatsu Airport and have them ready the jet! And, you, stay here and capture the girl."

"U-understood!"

After relaying his orders, Watanabe dashed around to the entrance and retrieved his footwear. Unwilling to put his Italian leather shoes on with muddy socks, he leaped into the sedan and drove away in a hurry, leaving one of his minions behind.

Morio heard a car's engine revving and turned toward the entrance to look.

Come to think of it, there was a strange car parked outside Kokone's home. Was it that one? he wondered. He heard a door sliding open and the sound of something heavy dropping to the floor behind him. He turned around and saw Kokone tumble from the closet, her skirt peeled up to her butt.

"What are you doing? I can see your underwear."

What was a high schooler doing in the closet? This girl made no sense. While Morio rolled his eyes, Kokone hastily fixed her skirt.

"Heh, nothing!" Her cheeks reddened. She grabbed Morio's outstretched hand almost instinctively and, her expression suddenly serious, pulled him toward the garage.

"Morio, can you ride a motorcycle?"

"Huh? That's kinda sudden."

It was Morio's turn to panic. Kokone had dragged him outside, and there stood an old S-193 Heart, a sidecar-mounted motorcycle by Shijima Motors that Momotarou had been in the process of customizing. Dazed, Morio did nothing.

"Well? Can you?"

"I only have an ordinary driver's license!" Morio protested.

"That's fine!" Kokone gave him her seal of approval and, as if she knew exactly what she was doing, turned the ignition key, put her foot on the starter, and pushed as hard as she could. The flat engine started up with a distinctive *vroom*.

"Drive."

"Wha—?!"

Without waiting for Morio to reply, Kokone took a helmet from the sidecar, put it on, and hopped in.

"It's all right! You can ride one of these with a regular license. Destination, Takamatsu Airport!"

Morio knew all too well how his stubborn childhood friend took after her father. He climbed onto the seat, muttering his grievances, and squeezed the clutch. The motorcycle revved. He had memories of riding it with Kokone as a child, when Momotarou was driving. But never had he expected to drive an artifact like this.

"Come on, more!"

As Kokone yelled over the engine, a man in sunglasses and a black suit appeared in the entrance of the garage.

"You two!"

When he saw the man, clearly not a friend, Morio inadvertently released the clutch. The roaring bike accelerated, and its front wheel rose up into the air.

"Whoa!"

The bike narrowly avoided hitting the man—or more accurately, the man dodged—and sped away without incident, still accelerating.

"Whoo, go, Morio!" Kokone cheered.

Meanwhile, Momotarou was in the police station's interrogation room.

Thanks to the police car and airplane waiting for him, he'd arrived in Tokyo almost too smoothly.

He had never even thought of coming back to this city until that morning.

He had been sitting in the interrogation room alone for a while—he had no idea what the police were up to. He crossed his legs and leaned back, then took a look at his phone, which he had covertly kept. The phone displayed his message to Kokone: "*I left the tablet at the grave. Don't let them have it.*"

He wondered whether Kokone had gone to the grave. Whether she had noticed Joy or the tablet inside. His message had been received, but she hadn't yet responded.

It was inconceivable that the phone-loving Kokone would take so long to respond, unlike him. She might just be mad, or something might have happened to her. Did she even know he had been arrested?

Maybe she was sleepy since he'd let her play mahjong yesterday, and she had just left his message for later... But considering his current predicament, it seemed unlikely that nobody would have contacted her yet. If Watanabe had captured her...

A myriad of worries flooded his brain. Though usually imperturbable, he was prone to excessive concern once he got started. Momotarou had always disliked that about himself.

The room's doorknob began slowly turning. Momotarou quickly hid his cell phone, and just as he did, two officers came into the room.

"...Did you just hide something?" An older officer, Tsukamoto, glared sharply at Momotarou.

"Nah," Momotarou replied, a fearless smile on his face. He stood in front of the two and pulled out his pants pockets, revealing that they contained nothing. Officer Tsukamoto's suspicions were clearly not alleviated.

"I swear."

"Koyama!"

"Yes, sir... I'm going to search you," Officer Koyama said to Momotarou.

At Officer Tsukamoto's behest, the young policeman searched Momotarou's pants pockets, his waist, and his crotch. The search revealed nothing.

"I told you, Koyama."

After so many searches for cigarettes by safety officers in high school, Momotarou had perfected the art of dropping contraband through holes in his pants pockets and into the cuffs.

Too easy...

Momotarou passed the search effortlessly.

Kokone got Morio up to speed on their way across the Great Seto Bridge. Her explanation was clumsy, though, which suggested she hadn't completely digested the information herself.

According to her, an unsavory bearded man had appeared at

Kokone's home in search of a tablet and then stolen her late mother's plushie because it contained what he was looking for. Then Kokone had apparently hidden in the closet because the man also planned to kidnap her.

"Am I really supposed to believe that?"

"But it's true! You saw the man in sunglasses, too, didn't you?"

He had, in fact, and he thought the man could have something to do with Momotarou's recent arrest, too. But the situation, apparently involving kidnapping and robbery, was too much for him—he was just an ordinary college student. When it came to people who might be reliable in circumstances like these, he first thought of his father. He then reconsidered, doubting the wisdom in relying on a biker gang of forty-year-olds calling themselves the Momotarous, but he ultimately concluded they might benefit from contacting Kijita, the policeman.

"...Shouldn't we contact Mr. Kijita?"

"We can't!"

An instant no... Morio realized his opinions were worthless in this relationship. To be fair, that had always been the case.

"We need to recover Joy and the tablet first; they'll get away otherwise. We'll contact Mr. Kijita after!"

Morio had always thought Kokone was like a cat: She would normally take a nap every chance she got, but when provoked, she would persevere until her battery ran dry.

Morio glanced at Kokone out of the corner of his eye, still facing ahead. Noting her sharp concentration on what they should do next, Morio remembered to focus on the road, closed his mouth, and sped up.

Watanabe arrived at Takamatsu Airport just as the plane was getting ready to leave, checked in, and hurried toward the gate. He held a Zero Halliburton–brand attaché case and Joy stuffed into a burlap bag. The plushie's head protruded from the bag, which was rather embarrassing for a businessman in an Italian suit about to board a private jet.

Kokone and Morio arrived at the airport a few minutes later. Kokone leaped from the bike as it was slowing down and took her helmet off.

"Keep the engine running and wait here!" she said before running off toward the entrance.

"Hey, Kokone!" Morio yelled after her, to no avail. "Man, she really is a cat."

Kokone surveyed the airport from behind the greenery planted around its entrance. Then, as luck would have it, she saw Watanabe conversing with an employee at a counter.

"There he is…"

It was past eight in the evening, so the airport was sparsely populated. Had Watanabe turned in Kokone's direction, he probably would have spotted her immediately. After a few moments of observation, Kokone saw him give an order to his underling, who bowed to him and scurried off. At Watanabe's feet were an attaché case and Joy sticking out of a bag. Perfect.

Takamatsu Airport's lobby was small—only about eighty yards from the entrance to the check-in desk. As two passengers walked in dragging suitcases through the automatic doors, Kokone followed them and hid behind a bulletin board. Now there were only fifty-five yards to Watanabe. She shifted, preparing to get even closer, when the rubber soles of the sneakers she had put on in the garage made a squeaking noise. Kokone took them off and, now in her socks, crouched down and approached.

Consulting his phone, Watanabe began filling out a form. Kokone closed in while he was preoccupied, hooked the strap of the bag containing Joy to her hand, and tugged it closer. But the bag's drawstring was tied to the attaché case—Kokone could not pull it free.

"!"

Watanabe was still wary, it seemed.

After a moment of fear, Kokone decided she didn't have time to waste. She seized his luggage, attaché case and all, and crept back to the shadow of the bulletin board. She turned around, but Watanabe seemed to be still completing a form. She breathed a sigh of relief and started putting her sneakers back on.

"Mr. Watanabe! Your bag!" His underling had just returned from purchasing drinks on the second floor.

"?!"

Watanabe couldn't process what had happened for a second. He realized what his underling was referring to and looked down to find that his attaché case and the drawstring bag were gone.

Panicked, he searched for the culprit. He saw a girl dash through the automatic doors and toward the entrance. It was Kokone Morikawa, Momotarou's daughter.

"Why is she here?!"

As Kokone had ordered, Morio was sitting on the idling bike when he saw Kokone running in his direction with some luggage in her arms.

"Go around!" she called, sprinting past him.

"Huh?!"

She ran through a gap in the greenery and into the parking lot. Watanabe and his minion chased after her, not even noticing Morio.

"Now I see."

Morio, realizing what Kokone was up to, started forward on the bike.

Kokone cut diagonally across the parking lot. When they'd arrived, she'd noticed the motorway extended all around the property.

If Morio had understood what she had meant, she should be able to make her escape.

Kokone glanced behind her. Her two pursuers rounded a parked car and came after her.

"Oh, you must be Kokone Morikawa! We need to talk." Apparently having determined he couldn't catch her, Watanabe called out to her with feigned friendliness.

Without giving him the slightest response or breaking stride, Kokone bounded over the metal fence separating the parking lot from the flora with the grace of a hurdler and raced down the slight slope. Kokone had been running up and down hills and stone steps ever since she was a child, so the soft grass was as easy to navigate as a running track. She glided over the greenery and arrived at the road below—but Morio was nowhere to be seen. Kokone could see Watanabe tentatively making his way down. At this rate, they would catch up.

Just then, Morio turned the corner on the motorcycle.

"Kokone!"

"Good going, Morio!"

Morio slowed slightly. Kokone tossed the bags into the sidecar before hopping in herself.

"Stop right there!" yelled Watanabe. He instantly gave chase, but he missed them by a hair. Morio twisted the throttle as far as it would go, and the accelerating motorcycle left Watanabe's shout in the dust.

Kokone was relieved to see Watanabe shrinking in the distance, slowing down and yelling in vain.

"That's Gruff Track's daughter for you!"

As the motorcycle gained speed, Morio's praise for his fearless childhood friend came from the heart.

"Damn it... Delay the flight! We need to capture that girl!"

Watanabe, exhausted and panting, took his phone out and called the subordinate he had left at the Morikawa household.

"It's me. Why is the girl here?"

"I, uh… I tried to catch her, but she got away, sir…," the other man said, clearly uncomfortable.

Unable to hide his irritation, Watanabe thundered, "You idiot! Why didn't you contact me immediately?!"

"I thought you might, um, yell at me…"

Useless, the lot of them!

Before frustration at the man's grade-school-level reasoning could give him an aneurysm, Watanabe swallowed his fury and regained his composure.

"Tell the police that Momotarou has a phone hidden on his person."

Sensing that things were about to get difficult, Watanabe loosened his necktie with his free hand and undid the buttons on his jacket.

Momotarou and Kokone Morikawa—how dare you make a fool of me!

"Request backup from the police over here, as well. Tell them the suspect's daughter is fleeing with evidence."

Watanabe turned his phone off and stuck it in his breast pocket, then pulled Kokone's from his jacket. He stared at the display, still showing Momotarou's message:

"If this man shows up, he's a bad guy." Simple. And an old photo.

The picture had been taken in Oota, at a subsidiary electronics company of Shijima's.

Watanabe reminisced. He and Momotarou had still been young then; their faces were full of hope. Ikumi was holding the dog plushie that had been in his own hands mere minutes ago. He was grateful for the opportunity to corner the company's chairman, but he hadn't expected to have to deal with Momotarou and Ikumi's daughter more than seventeen years down the line.

Watanabe suppressed his frustration and began plotting to take back the tablet.

*   *   *

Kokone and Morio rode across the Seto Chuo Expressway toward the Great Seto Bridge.

"I'm so glad you're okay, Joy…" She hugged the plushie to her chest as a mother might hold her child. In truth, it was also a way of containing the quivers of excitement coursing through her, but either way, she was hugging Joy tightly.

"She was my mom's," Kokone mumbled once the shivers subsided. Normally, she didn't think about her mother's absence often, but after she had almost lost Joy, her deceased parent was now at the forefront of her thoughts.

Kokone gave Joy another hug, then pulled the zipper open and made sure the tablet was there. She smiled in elation at successfully keeping it from the "bad guy," as her father had instructed, and at beating the unsavory bearded man.

Just then, Morio slowed down. Kokone wondered why but soon saw the reason—a police car was racing toward them from behind at top speed. Kokone could tell from Morio's expression that he hadn't been speeding. So why were the police after them?

But despite Kokone's concerns, the police car sped past the motorcycle. The two looked at each other.

"You think that bearded guy did something?"

"We would've been caught if so. He saw our motorcycle." Morio wasn't so sure. "But y'know, the police in the country are pretty chill. We might've just gotten lucky."

Kokone thought he might be onto something. The police over here were indeed *pretty chill*.

Just in case, though, the two decided to get off the highway.

Morio took the last exit before the highway led them out of Shikoku toward Marugame, but without much knowledge of the area or streetlights to guide his way, he struggled to make progress through the country's roads. Kokone told him to stop the motorcycle, so Morio stopped at a small shrine next to a field in the middle of nowhere and cut the engine.

Kokone took off her helmet and climbed out of the sidecar, stretching to loosen up after sitting for so long.

"Morio, lend me your phone."

It was summer, but riding a motorbike at night with only a polo shirt on had chilled Kokone to the core, and she instinctively rubbed her arms to warm up. "Let's contact Mr. Kijita and have him pick us up in his police car."

"Wha…?! You keep coming up with one crazy plan after another, you know that?" Morio was surprised and exasperated. "He's a policeman. We'll be caught if we do that."

Although her plan made sense, it was still flawed, in Morio's opinion, but he handed Kokone his phone anyway. He then removed his jacket and lent it to her. Kokone gratefully put it on and handed Momotarou's tablet to Morio in exchange.

"I'm wondering if there's a way we can contact Dad with this. They took my phone, and I don't remember his e-mail or anything," she said.

Morio had seen the tablet before. It was an old model with a crack in the middle. What had the bearded man wanted with something like this? Still wondering, Morio swiped across the screen, which didn't even ask for a password.

Kokone called Kijita on Morio's phone as she walked along a nearby field.

"Hi, Mr. Kijita? …Yeah, I'm with Morio. Something happened, and we're in Takamatsu right now. We were kinda hoping you'd come pick us up."

Kijita admonished Kokone for leaving home with Morio when her father had been arrested only that morning, but she explained that she had chased a mysterious man who might be connected with her father's arrest to Takamatsu Airport. Kijita immediately pursued that line of questioning. The loyalty of the Momotarous apparently hadn't changed since the group was formed in high school.

"That's a big deal, Kokone. I'll be right there."

Kokone pushed for Kijita to come in his police car, but he declined—he couldn't drive it in civilian clothing. Even so, the prospect of help from a powerful ally gave Kokone newfound energy, and she began entertaining the idea of actually rescuing Momotarou soon.

Morio had since relocated to the motorcycle's back and was silently inspecting the tablet. He figured the applications were more or less ordered by frequency of usage. He tapped each icon and closed it once he knew what the app did. Unsurprisingly, given Momotarou's hobby of modding cars, there were multiple applications for diagnosing the computers of various makers of cars—scanner-reader software. Among them were a few illegal apps.

"So he was using it primarily as a scanner-reader for cars…"

To Morio, Shimotsui's first genius and current student of Tokyo Institute of Technology, the device seemed cheaply constructed, but considering its custom-made programs, perhaps it did contain something worth stealing.

"What do you think? Can we get in touch with Dad?" Kokone asked, handing Morio his phone.

Morio returned the phone to his pocket. "This tablet was used to determine what condition cars are in and stuff, but there's no address book inside. It is connected to the Internet, but…"

Morio minimized the program and showed Kokone the home screen.

"Oh…"

"Doesn't Mr. Kijita know Uncle Momo's e-mail?"

"They see each other all the time; they don't use e-mail."

"I see…"

Even the quiet Momotarou was talkative with his buddies, and they were all neighbors. They often gathered to play mahjong and drink, so they didn't need things like e-mail.

"Huh? …What's this?" Morio, who had been swiping across the home screen to show Kokone the apps, paused when he found an unfamiliar icon on the last screen. The icon was a skull, and the app was named A-HEART. There was a red "1" on the upper-left corner of the icon, indicating a notification. Morio tapped the app, and a "timeline" popped up with short paragraphs apparently written by various individuals.

The name Momotarou was among them.

"Is this Dad…?"

"Yeah… Looks like this app is for a secret social networking site where people swap info about car mods." *This might be another custom program…*, Morio hypothesized. "If we leave a message on this timeline, Uncle Momo might read it on his phone," he said, scrolling down and skimming the messages.

Kokone broke into a smile. "Perfect!"

She took the tablet from Morio and started typing messages to her father.

"You okay, Dad?"

"Where are you?"

"The bearded man came."

"Took the tablet and my phone, got the tablet back. Can't send e-mails, so wrote here. Kokone."

Kokone typed cheerfully and then tapped the screen. "Enter!"

Watching her, Morio couldn't help but wonder again. "…Why did they come after this tablet?"

Kokone's expression read *One down* as she lifted her face from the tablet.

"Dunno."

Well, no surprises there..., Morio muttered in his head.

Meanwhile, Momotarou waited wordlessly in the interrogation room with an expression of total confidence.

He knew from his days as a delinquent that the police hated it most when their questioning didn't lead to the answer they wanted. This was why he had successfully confused them by not even attempting to dispel their accusations.

"They usually make such a big deal of denying it when we accuse them..." As a veteran, Officer Tsukamoto was confounded by Momotarou's shameless attitude. However, the younger Koyama interpreted Momotarou's air of confidence as impudence and was determined to find a way to undo him.

Just then, the e-mail from Watanabe's assistant came. "*Morikawa is hiding a cell phone on his person.*"

Koyama devised a plan to outfox Momotarou then. After whispering into Tsukamoto's ear, he glanced in Momotarou's direction and slowly left the room.

Momotarou made sure that the two were gone before pulling out his phone from the cuff of his pants. He checked his messaging app, but no reply had come. Had something happened to Kokone, then? Annoyed, Momotarou swiped to the home screen. He saw that his social networking app, which he didn't often use outside of work, had a notification—from himself, strangely enough.

"Hmm...?"

He looked at it and saw that it was a message from Kokone.

That short paragraph was all he needed. Now that he knew what had happened to her, he relaxed a bit, but anger toward Watanabe was boiling inside him.

"That bastard! He'd better not have done anything to Kokone! He won't get away with it if he has!"

For an instant, Momotarou had forgotten that the police even existed, and that was when Koyama and Tsukamoto burst through the door.

"…I see how it is," Koyama spat, grabbing Momotarou's arm and wresting the phone from him.

I screwed up, thought Momotarou as he pulled his arm free. He pouted and crossed his arms, barely managing to control himself.

"We got a message from Shijima…," Koyama said, scrolling the phone's screen to read Kokone's message. "It seems your daughter is on the run with the tablet."

"She is?" Momotarou asked.

What did he mean by "on the run"?

"Why don't you tell your daughter to return what she stole?" Officer Tsukamoto said.

At that, Momotarou's self-control went up in smoke.

"Come on!" Momotarou slammed his hands on the desk. "…Shijima is the one trying to steal it! Even if he tries to copy it, the data will just disappear. He wants it 'cause he doesn't have the original!"

Screwed up again, thought Momotarou, but it was too late. Realizing he had fallen right into the cops' trap, Momotarou ruffled his hair in frustration.

"Whatcha doin'?" Kokone asked.

Morio had opened Watanabe's bag and started rifling through its contents.

"Hmm? I'm looking for something that'll tell me who that man was," he replied, then handed Kokone a business card.

"Shijima Motors… How do you read this?" Kanji characters were not Kokone's strong suit, and although she could read the name of the company, she had trouble with the job title.

"Are you sure you're in your third year of high school? Shijima Motors, director and senior management executive officer, Ichiro Watanabe… Wait, he works for Shijima Motors?!"

A driver's license belonging to an "Ichiro Watanabe" found in the same bag confirmed that the bearded man was, indeed, the director of the famous fifty-year-old company.

"What's Shijima Motors?"

It meant nothing to Kokone. Morio wondered whether his childhood friend was actually this oblivious to everything but her home and school life.

"Shijima is one of the biggest car manufacturers in Japan," Morio exasperatedly explained. He pointed a finger at the logo on their motorcycle. It was, in fact, made by Shijima Motors. The S-193 Heart. The first vehicle Shijima had ever produced. "How do you not know that?"

But Kokone showed no sign of comprehending. "I mean, *we're* Morikawa Motors. So…"

"Geez." Morio gave up on explaining.

"…Hey, come to think of it…"

"What?" Morio had started analyzing Watanabe's criminal actions instead, but Kokone cheerily interrupted him.

"I think my Mom's maiden name might have been Shijima!"

"…Huh…"

Kokone tee-heed at Morio's dumbfounded reaction. "Think that has anything to do with it?"

Ya think?! Morio mentally fired back. He quickly changed gears and, crossing his arms, fell deep into thought with a complicated expression.

"…How did your mother die, Kokone?"

"Um? I heard she died in an accident…"

Morio put a hand to his lips and mulled over what they knew. Kokone let out a big yawn next to him. Who that bearded guy was, Shijima Motors, her late mother... All these problems were overwhelming for her mind to process, and drowsiness overtook her before she could arrive at an explanation.

"I'm gonna sleep until Mr. Kijita gets here. Nothing to do." Kokone climbed off the bike and wriggled into the sidecar, where Morio was sitting.

"Huh?! Now?" Morio answered—partly disapproving, partly confused—but Kokone paid no attention, leaned back in the seat, and closed her eyes.

She reopened them immediately. "...You can stay here because it's cold, but don't touch my butt."

"! L-like I would..." Morio hadn't been considering it, but now that she'd mentioned it, he couldn't help his quickening pulse. His cheeks reddening, Morio attempted to put some space between him and Kokone, but there wasn't enough room in the sidecar for that. Like it or not, their bodies were pressed together in the cramped interior. Morio looked uncomfortably in Kokone's direction, but she was already in a deep sleep, snoring softly. Her face was so peaceful, you'd never guess what a turbulent and mystery-packed day it had been.

What good could it do for me to worry about this if she isn't concerned?

Morio took off his glasses, lay down facing away from Kokone, and gently closed his eyes.

*   *   *

A large full moon hung in the sky and bathed the world in a blue-white glow, not unlike a snowy evening. Morio, who had lent his jacket to Kokone, was awoken by a chill in his stomach and opened his eyes. His eyelids protested, but he forced them open and put his glasses on. He saw a torii gate in front of him.

Man, it's really bright... The contrast between the brightly shining torii gate and the dark shadow it cast was unsettling. He turned around, and his jaw dropped at what he saw. There, where he had expected to see a rural landscape glowing in the morning sunlight, was instead a placid sea reflecting the night sky. And Kokone, who should have been sleeping next to him, was no longer there.

Morio climbed out of the sidecar to look for her and saw a human silhouette in the distance.

"...Kokone?!"

Morio timidly approached. As he neared the figure, he saw that it belonged to a little girl dressed like a pirate, and next to her, Joy was walking on its own.

"That plushie's walking by itself!"

"Morio? Why are you here?" It seemed the girl knew him.

"Huh? Who are you?" asked Morio apprehensively.

The little girl was equally nervous as she replied, "I'm Ancien! ... Um, but really, I'm Kokone."

"Wha...?"

When he looked closer, she did, in fact, resemble a young Kokone. Ancien seemed unsure what to say to Morio's skepticism. Joy watched the two with uncertainty.

In an attempt to comprehend the situation, Morio scanned their whereabouts again. He was certain he had fallen asleep in the grove of a village shrine, but now he seemed to be on a small island in the middle of the ocean.

"I think this is somewhere on Hill Mountain, but..."

"Hill Mountain?"

While Ancien and Morio warily continued their conversation, two men came running up the coast. One was wearing a smelting mask, and the other had a bird-themed masquerade mask.

"Terrible news!" yelled one of them in a voice Morio recognized from somewhere.

The two stopped in front of Ancien and took off their masks. Their faces belonged to Kijita and Morio's own father, Sawatari.

"Mr. Kijita! …Dad?!"

The two were dressed like soldiers for some reason and looked much younger than they should have.

Irritated, Sawatari glared at Morio. "Who's this nincompoop?" he demanded angrily.

"What? Did you forget what your own son looks like?"

"Huh? I don't remember having a son as old as you!"

While the two argued, Kijita regretfully relayed his news to Ancien.

"Ancien, Bewan has captured Peach."

"Huh?!"

Sawatari composed himself and added, "Soldiers are on their way here, too."

"Leave this to us and go save Peach!"

Having said that, the two donned their masks again and ran back in the direction they had come.

"…Awfully young, weren't they…?"

While Morio was distracted by that irrelevant detail, Ancien called, "Morio, let's go!"

"What?!"

"If we save Dad in this dream, maybe we can rescue him in real life, too!"

Ancien dashed off toward Heart, and Morio followed. With a serious expression, Joy grunted in agreement and raced after them.

"Hey, hold on. What do you mean, a dream?!"

"I've been having dreams since this morning that are connected to reality, somehow. It'll be easier to save Dad over here, where I can use magic!" Ancien explained with frustration, jumping into the sidecar.

Morio climbed onto the motorcycle and started the engine, just as he had in real life. The motorcycle raced forward at a tremendous speed.

After they had traveled some distance along the coast, the two were able to see Kijita and Sawatari fighting against the soldiers in shallow water.

Ancien waved her hand at the two. "Takiji! Ukki! I'll leave it to you!" she called. Then, with joy rather than concern, she gave orders to her new companion. "Morio, to the air!"

"Huh…?!"

There was a sudden clunk, and it felt as though the chassis was sinking into the ground. But a second later, its wheels floated into the air, and the motorcycle, sidecar and all, gained altitude and flew off into the sky like a plane.

"Whoaaa!"

The motorcycle rose farther from the ground, and the figures of Takiji and Ukki in their fight shrank. Morio watched the two challenging dozens of soldiers with nothing but themselves and their swords, and he wondered whether that was how they had been back in their delinquent days. He couldn't help but feel a pang of pride.

Suddenly, the motorcycle started shaking violently and, as if it had just remembered the existence of gravity, began accelerating toward the ground.

"Heart, what's wrong?" Heart wasn't back to 100 percent yet, but still Kokone cheered it on.

Then, moments before they were about to crash, the motorcycle halted its descent just above the water and started skimming along its surface, as if intending to cut through the mass of soldiers attacking Takiji and Ukki.

"Outta the way!" shrieked Morio and Ancien.

Ukki raised his sword toward them. "Ancien! Peach is in your hands!"

"Leave it to me!" Ancien held her straw hat to her head to keep it from blowing away and gave them a wave and a smile.

Morio and Ancien zipped away from the island across the surface of the calm sea.

"…How is this happening…?" wondered Morio.

Heart began floating up again without a trace of its prior uncertainty and sped upward. A large full moon hung in front of them, and a bridge reminiscent of the Great Seto Bridge stretched all the way across the horizon. The wheels of Morio's mind slowed to a halt before the awe-inspiring view, and Ancien began explaining this world's workings to him.

"This is a fairy-tale world that Dad made up long ago."

"A fairy-tale world?"

"Yeah. Don't you remember, Morio? He used to tell us bedtime stories when you came over."

Morio tried hard to recall the childhood memory.

"…Come to think of it, I do remember Uncle Momo used to make up stories about a princess."

"They were so fun… Can't imagine him doing that now, though," Ancien muttered with some chagrin.

"You were always asleep, though," Morio teased.

"Wait, really?" Ancien scratched her head bashfully. She did seem to remember that.

Little by little, Morio connected the dots between the fairy tale from his memory and reality.

"…I see now. They're the Momotarous. They're the monkey and the pheasant, so they're named Ukki and Takiji. *Momo* means 'peach,' so that's self-explanatory. But why does Kokone become Ancien?" Morio was delighted to find that his memories were returning. "It must be because everybody is as they were back then."

"Then why are you still Morio, Morio?"

Joy piped up to answer this one. "Morio has never appeared in these stories, so he doesn't have a dream version."

Morio was surprised that Joy could not only walk but speak.

"Oh, really?" Ancien was a little disappointed to learn that Morio had no place here, even though he'd enjoyed the tales so much in the past.

But Morio didn't seem disappointed at all—if anything, he was having a blast making hypotheses about this dream.

"If so, then I'm nothing more than the 'Morio' of your dreams. When you wake up, the real Morio won't remember your dream at all."

Morio seemed to be fine with this, but Ancien's disappointment only grew. "Aw, that sucks! Where's the magic in that?"

"You'll have to just accept it. I'm a realist," Morio replied, then firmly gripped Heart's handlebars and turned them hard. Leaning far to the side, Heart swerved and flew under and away from the long bridge. Then Heart did an about-face and zoomed under the bridge's arch, grazing its cables, and accelerated.

It seemed that Morio was getting the hang of riding Heart in this world. They plunged like an intense roller coaster into a cloud, tearing through a tunnel of fog. Vapor trails wisped from the motorcycle and sidecar's edges, and Ancien's eyes widened.

"The water in the air is turning into vapor because of the change in pressure. Put your hand out, Kokone."

Ancien did as Morio instructed and extended her right hand, and the wisps trailed from her fingertips, too.

"What is this? It's so neat!" Ancien exclaimed at the ever-changing sights, grinning with delight.

Even Morio, who had called himself a realist minutes before, seemed to be genuinely enjoying the ethereal world around him. But bad things tend to happen when you get carried away.

"Whoa!"

The two had evidently lost their sense of direction in the cloud, and suddenly, one of the bridge's pillars was right in front of them. The motorcycle's back wheel just barely made contact with the bridge, and the impact loosened Morio's grip on the bars. He was hurled from the motorcycle and through the cloud into the open sky. Ancien quickly transformed Heart back into humanoid form and dived to save Morio.

"Aaaaaaah!" *Is this how I'm gonna die? But this is Kokone's dream.*

Even if he did die, the real him would still be alive, as if nothing had happened. Still, telling himself this did nothing to soothe his terror.

This might be the end… Just as he braced himself, Heart's robot arm grabbed him.

"…Too close…"

With Ancien and Joy on its back and Morio in its arms, Heart soared through the deep, dark night sky toward a shining, jewellike town. Ancien let out a gasp in awe of its beauty.

"…Oh, right." Morio had remembered something while he was watching the landscape below with Ancien. "The title was 'Ancien and the Magic Tablet.'"

The title belonged to the fairy tale Momotarou had told Kokone in her youth.

"You're right! 'Ancien and the Magic Tablet'!" Ancien repeated joyfully.

The two shared a smile. At that moment, Heart shuddered again.

"Ah! What is it this time?!" yelped Morio. The unstable movement wasn't just a loss of balance.

Ancien noticed that the fuel gauge on Heart's back read *Empty*.

"Out of gas?!"

"No way!!"

Ancien desperately clung to the bucking motorcycle and ordered, "Heart, land somewhere!"

Unresponsive, Heart tumbled out of the night sky toward the sparkling town.

"Waaaaaah!"

"Aaaaaah!"

Morio, Ancien, and Joy could do nothing but scream. They squeezed their eyes shut and braced themselves for impact.

Chapter 3

* * *

"…aaah!"

As if she was trying to escape the breakneck fall in her dream, Kokone's eyes snapped open.

The unpleasant, stuffy smell of heat, food, exhaust, and ammonia washed over her. The torii gate and the grove that should have been in front of her had disappeared, and a concrete wall arched over her head. *An underpass tunnel…?* Morio was nowhere to be found, either. Panicking, she turned around and found him standing a distance away from her. They had apparently come here with Heart during her dream about flying with Morio. Kokone crept out from the sidecar and walked toward her friend.

"Morio! Where are we?"

Though her vision was still blurred from sleep, Kokone saw a legion of skyscrapers lining stagnant waterways and a giant, gaudy billboard. The formidable sight overwhelmed her.

Apparently feeling the same, Morio simply stood there, too, limp and wide-eyed.

The pink light of day shone through the cracks between the

buildings and illuminated the Asahi Beer billboard. It must have been roughly five in the morning.

Morio managed to pull himself together and rasp, "This is… Doutonbori, in Osaka."

He pointed at the wall of a building, where the LED of a giant Glico billboard shone down on Kokone.

The two pulled their motorcycle from the tunnel. Its gas tank, almost full the night before, was now empty, and pushing its heavy chassis was a struggle even for the two of them together.

"…I mean, we were just waiting for the Momotarous at Takamatsu, dreaming about flying on a motorcycle…," Morio commented quietly once they had pushed Heart onto a sidewalk.

"Huh?! You had the same dream?"

"Same dream?"

Kokone had assumed that, as the dream Morio had said, the real Morio would know nothing about the dream at all, much less remember it. But he had been the one to bring it up…

Suddenly elated, Kokone peered into Morio's face.

"All right! It's just like magic!"

Morio had realized the importance of studying in middle school, and he had always made fun of Kokone's dreamy comments that flew in the face of logic—but this time, Morio had mentioned the shared dream. *Told you so*, thought Kokone. Sometimes, real life could be surreal, too.

Kokone flung her arms into the air in an outburst of delight.

"Stop that!" Morio said. "You're in high school…"

But those words wouldn't reach her now. Excited that her dream had somehow linked her and Morio, Kokone couldn't have cared less about appearances, and she sprinted along the stream to begin the adventure in real life.

"Are you a grade-schooler...?" Morio shook his head at the emotionally driven Kokone and began searching for clues as to what had happened. "The empty gas tank could mean somebody rode the bike while we were asleep..."

He didn't remember what the odometer had said earlier, but the motorcycle's computer should have some sort of record. Though it was an old model, Morio knew Momotarou had installed a satnav on it. He activated the navigation feature and checked for any records. Ordinarily, the start-up menu should have appeared, but instead it read *Autopilot: Active.*

"Huh?! Autopilot?"

Skeptical, Morio changed the screen to the map, which displayed a route from Takamatsu to Osaka, and after another tap, the screen read *Please Refuel.*

Did this old motorcycle drive them all the way here of its own accord?

Morio inspected the motorcycle more closely and was surprised to find that the complex motor underneath was directly connected to a computer, and that electrical wires and axles extended from it to the wheels. Not only that, but attached to the motorcycle's hood was a spherical camera and sensor designed to monitor the surrounding area in conjunction with GPS.

"Were we on the highway all night while we were sleeping?!" Morio could hardly believe it, but imagining them asleep on the highway, he felt a shiver go up his spine. But they had indeed flown over the Great Seto Bridge on the dream motorcycle as well. It could be that the motorcycle had started moving on its own in an effort to save Momotarou in real life and had run out of gas.

"...If so, then Uncle Momo's modifications aren't so silly after all—they're downright revolutionary..."

Web-based companies and automobile manufacturers worldwide

were in competition to develop self-driving cars. Japan, previously one of the world's great auto-manufacturing countries, had aimed to release this technology by the Tokyo Olympics in an effort to keep up with other countries, and it had brought domestic automobile manufacturers together to develop it. However, there were rumors that the technology was still incomplete, and Morio couldn't believe that a former delinquent with a small auto shop in the countryside could have developed it himself.

"The Momotarous did know a thing or two about engines, for sure. I'll give them that, but..." Morio inspected what had been the robot Heart's head in the dream world. "The hardware is one thing, but I doubt that Uncle Momo could have written such a complex program by himself."

The Momotarou Morio knew was a mechanic who silently took engines apart and put them back together. He knew some things about circuitry and electronics, but he'd certainly never seemed to be the programmer type.

Once his train of thought had reached that point, Morio directed his gaze to the tablet and Joy, both placed carefully on the sidecar's seat.

"Do you know how Uncle Momo used this tablet?"

But Joy, who had so articulately explained the mechanisms of his dream last night, said nothing.

"Morio!"

"Huh?"

Morio was crouched at the front of the sidecar, lost in thought until Kokone returned and pulled him back to reality.

Kokone pointed wordlessly at the top of the bridge behind Morio. A policeman was glaring at him—the motorcycle was stopped smack in front of a No Parking sign.

"S-sorry! It ran out of gas last night..." Morio smiled stiffly, then hurriedly tugged the motorcycle away from the sign.

*   *   *

Kokone and Morio pushed the motorcycle-turned-hunk-of-iron, in search of a gas station that was open in the morning, and they finally found one after a mile or two. Being more of an indoors, science type of person, Morio was exhausted, while Kokone hadn't broken a sweat. She operated the self-service machine and handed him a ten-thousand-yen bill.

"Pay for the gas with this, would you?" she said, then took the burlap bag containing Joy and the tablet to the waiting room.

Doesn't hesitate to use me, does she? Bet she can ride this motorcycle just fine herself, he thought, watching her go before he started pumping the gas.

Kokone checked Momotarou's tablet in the air-conditioned waiting room.

"I wonder if Dad's read my message..."

Momotarou had not replied to her note on the social networking app last night. It had no "read" feature, so there was no way of knowing whether he had even seen it. Anxious, Kokone decided to write another message to her father.

"'Where are you, Dad? I haven't given them the tablet, don't worry. We're refueling near Doutonbori.' And enter!"

Kokone stared at the screen, her cheeks puffed in frustration, but no reply came. She was getting less concerned about her father and more irritated at him for being lazy and not noticing her messages.

"C'mon, Dad, what are you doing...? Reply if you're okay, already!"

Morio finished refueling and replaced the nozzle. His phone rang. When he pulled it out of his pocket, he found multiple missed calls—all from his dad.

"...Hello?" He answered the phone as he headed toward the waiting room.

"Morio, where are you?" asked Sawatari.

"Um... Well..."

His old man didn't usually care what he did, but this was not a situation to be taken lightly. And no wonder his dad was worried—Morio had disappeared right after going to check on Kokone, whose father had been arrested that very morning. He wondered how best to explain that they were now in Osaka, but Sawatari asked before he could decide.

"Where did you go afterward? Kokone's with you, right?"

"Afterward?"

"Quit foolin' around. We went all the way to Takamatsu to pick you up, and you were nowhere to be found. Then we had a run-in with the police, and it turned into a huge mess!"

"Huh?" Morio answered in surprise. It was exactly like the dream.

When Morio didn't reply, Sawatari lowered his voice and said, "But never mind that. Let me speak to Kokone."

Despite his misgivings, Morio handed the phone to Kokone. "It's my old man."

"What is it?"

"Hi, Kokone. There's a real shady character over here right now…"

"Huh?" A certain man's face popped up in Kokone's head at the phrase *shady character*. "The guy with the beard?"

"Y-yeah… Him."

Yesterday, Sawatari had heard about Momotarou's arrest from Kijita, and he'd gone to the Morikawa home right after work was over. Morio had come to see her with a bento box, but they were both gone, and while Sawatari was busy wondering what had happened, Kijita had arrived. That was when Kokone had gotten in touch with Sawatari and told him to come pick them up in Takamatsu, so the two had headed for the shrine in Sawatari's car. But the kids hadn't been there, either. The local police had then come by and informed them they were looking for a girl who had stolen a tablet at Takamatsu Airport, and the conversation had turned into a fight. Sawatari and Kijita had both suspected the girl was Kokone, but they had said nothing. And this morning, the man claiming his tablet had been stolen had stopped by and was ordering them to return it.

"Kijita's talking to the bearded guy at the door right now." Sawatari was calling Kokone from a hiding place in the workshop. "He says he's here on behalf of your grandfather. Looks like there's something really complicated going on."

"But my grandpa died when I was in grade school."

"On Ikumi's side, not Momo's."

Kokone's eyes opened wide when she heard her mother's name. "My mom's?!"

"Yeah. I was surprised when I heard that, too. Sounds like your grandfather is the chairman of Shijima Motors."

Kokone gulped despite herself and looked at Morio, remembering their discussion the night before. "I think my mom's maiden name might have been Shijima…'"

Keeping an eye on Watanabe's behavior, Sawatari continued his conversation with Kokone from the workshop's corner. "It seems Momo had some good reasons for not talking about Ikumi."

"Like what?"

"Apparently, Uncle Momo and Ikumi eloped. After that, they were forced to promise not to have anything to do with the Shijima family whatsoever."

As Kokone learned the details of her parents' marriage, the story felt almost as if it were about total strangers.

"And yet he had the gall to steal data from Shijima, of all things."

"!"

While Sawatari and Kokone were talking, Watanabe had abruptly ended his conversation with Kijita and come into the house.

"My dad isn't a thief, you know," Kokone said with conviction. Her father often acted grumpy, spoke tactlessly, and created misunderstandings, but he hated injustice. Though he didn't trouble himself to do much parenting for Kokone, he had always taught her that while she was allowed to be mischievous, she should never steal. Kokone couldn't imagine he would ever rob someone.

But Watanabe scoffed. "I wonder," he coldly replied.

Sawatari took his phone back and said, "Kokone, we believe in Momo, too. But we need that tablet you have to prove his innocence."

"That's right," Watanabe said to both of them, fixing Sawatari with a glare. "If you hand over the tablet, Chairman Shijima will drop the charges. Otherwise…your father will be charged with a very serious crime." Watanabe smirked.

Kokone's expression was frozen, but she had inherited her father's stubbornness, so she did not mince words in her reply. "In that case, I'll meet with Chairman Shijima myself and prove to him that my dad isn't that kind of person!"

"Wh-what?!" Watanabe stammered, clearly panicking. "Th-the chairman won't see you!"

"Why not?"

"Because…he still holds a grudge against Morikawa."

Sawatari was astonished at how flustered Watanabe had become.

On the other hand, Kokone showed no signs of wavering. "But I'm this Shijima guy's granddaughter, right?"

"No, well… That's true, but…"

Kokone jumped to her feet with a *bam*. "My dad may be a former delinquent, and he may be kinda childish, but he does the right thing. And so will I! Good-bye!" She hung up.

Watanabe could only grind his teeth on the other end. "…Damn it. These Morikawas never do what I ask…" He jabbed a finger at Sawatari, who was not his subordinate, and shouted, "Hey, you! Call that girl back!"

"There's no point," Sawatari replied with a laugh. "Kokone's just like Momo. Once she's made up her mind, there's no convincing her otherwise."

Watanabe clicked his tongue. "Let's go," he snapped at his assistants. "This is why I hate these rubes…"

Kijita and Sawatari watched Watanabe leave and grinned at each other.

"…Nice work, Kokone."

"Yeah. She's Gruff Track's daughter, all right."

Kokone's anger didn't subside even after she returned Morio's phone to him.

"Everything in me is telling me not to like that bearded guy!"

After getting his phone back, Morio noticed something fishy happening in front of them.

"Hey, Kokone. Check him out…"

Their eyes locked with a pale-faced man in work clothes standing next to the gas pumps. Perhaps because Morio had spotted him, the man was suspiciously retreating to the side of the fat man standing behind him, presumably his companion. The fat man turned away in a panic, but Morio and Kokone could see the words SHIJIMA MOTORS OSAKA TECHNICAL RESEARCH FACILITY printed on the car beside them. The only reason people from Shijima would be there was Kokone and the tablet.

"…Beardy's friends, huh?"

"Gah! What'll we do?"

Morio had an epiphany. "Okay. Go to sleep, right now."

"Wait, why?"

"Why? You can use magic in your dreams, can't you?"

"Uh?! I mean, I can't right now. I just woke up."

"Like that would stop you. You're always sleeping." Morio was half joking, but Kokone was earnestly defending herself. *Seriously?* he thought, but he immediately started thinking of another plan. First, since the men were both focused on Kokone, Morio sneaked out of the waiting room alone. He crawled away from where they could see him and made his way to the fully fueled Heart. He tapped the motorcycle's autopilot menu screen and entered a destination.

"You go home without us."

If the motorcycle had driven itself all this way, then Heart should be able to drive back to Shimotsui unassisted.

Morio tapped the HOME button on the autopilot menu and started the engine. The motorcycle rolled forward.

With no passengers, Heart wheeled itself out of the gas station, turn signals flashing, and drove off at a safe pace.

"Go, Heart," Morio whispered from behind a pillar.

The two men, noticing that Heart had suddenly left the gas station, chased after it in a panic.

"Damn it!"

Once they were gone, Morio went to get Kokone from her hiding place in the waiting room.

As soon as she realized Heart was nowhere to be found, she worriedly asked him, "Where's Dad's bike?"

"Don't worry; trust me." He urged Kokone on despite her uncertainty, and the two ran in the opposite direction of Heart.

After a while, the men in work clothes returned to the gas station. The two didn't appear to get regular exercise. Shoulders heaving, they peered into the waiting room to find that Kokone and Morio had disappeared. Dismayed, they both pulled out their phones to contact someone.

Kokone and Morio hailed a taxi on one of the main roads and arrived at Shin Osaka Station about ten minutes later. Kokone paid the cab fare and chased after Morio, who had already run inside the station. Morio was inspecting the bullet-train timetables.

"Morio, do you have some money? I only have six hundred and fifty yen left."

"What?!" yelped Morio as he looked for an open seat.

Kokone had spent her money from mahjong on gasoline for Heart, the taxi fare, and highway tolls, among other things, so she was nearly broke.

"I don't have any!"

"But you're a college student. How do you not have any money?"

"I mean… Well, I was only stopping by yesterday, and besides, college guys don't have money these days. That's a given." A lack of funds wasn't something to be proud of, but he still stubbornly held that his lack of a part-time job was evidence of his dedication to his studies. He was proud of that, at least.

"How were you planning to get to Tokyo without Heart?" asked Kokone, perfectly oblivious to Morio's pride.

"I was relying on you to pay… Pretty shameless." He hung his head in apology.

Kokone sighed.

"I know! What if we use the beard guy's money?" Morio pointed at Watanabe's attaché case.

But Kokone immediately and firmly replied, "Nope. That'd be stealing!"

This was true, but Morio was pained to think Kokone insisted on adhering to her father's rigid morals even against an adversary who was already using underhanded methods.

"So what'll we do?"

As if to interrupt Morio's question, a notification sound chirped from the tablet in the sack on Kokone's back. She lowered the bag with Joy's head poking out and took out the device to check the app.

"It's from Dad!"

At long last, a reply from "Momotarou" had appeared on the timeline. Kokone's face brightened.

"*Where are you, Kokone?*"

The lone sentence suggested he wanted to hear about their situation before explaining his own.

"*We're at Shin Osaka Station. We're coming to rescue you.*" Kokone hastily wrote her response and sent it.

"*Stay there.*"

"Huh?!" yelped Kokone at the unexpected reply. Was he not telling them where he was because he didn't want to worry them?

"*I'm with Morio.*"

"*Don't have money, can't get on the bullet train.*"

Kokone gave him information about their situation, unable to do much else. This time, no reply came for a while. Getting impatient, she wrote again, "*Where are you, Dad?*"

After some time, the response came: "*Wait there.*"

"…?"

"…Something's off." Morio cocked his head. Momotarou had said nothing of his own situation and merely repeated his instructions to wait. Even if he was worried about Kokone, the lack of a detailed explanation or further directions was strange. The two stood there for a while, their heads full of question marks, until Kokone couldn't take it anymore and sent another message.

"*I want to go to Tokyo on the bullet train.*"

No response. Kokone *hmm*ed, and just then, a female train station employee came running up to them.

"Are you Kokone Morikawa?"

"Huh?"

Kokone started at the sound of her name. The woman held a small envelope out to Kokone and explained kindly, "We were asked to hold on to bullet-train tickets in your name."

"Huh?!" Kokone and Morio exclaimed. The envelope contained two reserved-seat tickets that read *Shin Osaka → Tokyo*.

"What…?"

"…Can you explain what's going on?" Morio asked the woman, perplexed. But the woman, equally puzzled, didn't seem to know, either. It was nearly time for the train on their tickets to depart, and Kokone decided to go for it rather than try to understand what was happening. She opened the envelope and handed a ticket to Morio, then picked up Watanabe's attaché from the ground and handed it to the employee.

"Somebody dropped this. Would you mind giving it to the police?" Kokone said, picking up the bag containing Joy and the tablet and making a dash for their train.

"H-hey!" Morio frantically chased after her. He slipped the ticket through the turnstile, snatched the stub out with annoyance, and sprinted up the stairs. Just as he made it to the platform, the departure bell rang shrilly. Kokone and Morio squeezed through the closing doors and into the car. As they caught their breath in the vestibule, the train departed for Tokyo.

When they found their designated seats, Kokone gently bounced herself on the cushions as if to test the springs.

"Wooow! It's my first time on a bullet train!"

Morio sat beside the hyperactive girl. *What is happening?* he wondered in tired amazement. They had gotten on the train without thinking, but they had no idea who had purchased these seats for them or why.

Kokone took Joy out of her bag and giddily asked, "You think this is magic, Joy?"

"But we're not in a dream." Morio wasn't so sure.

Kokone showed him the tablet. "But I texted 'I want to go to Tokyo,' and my wish came true!" she said, smiling. "…Lemme test it out again." She pulled up the social networking app. "'I'm hungry, and I want a bento box…' Enter!"

Morio was half-hopeful and half-bemused as he watched her innocent behavior, but lightning struck twice. The woman pushing the food cart stopped by and handed Kokone and Morio bento boxes, informing them that they had already been paid for, along with two bottles of tea.

"Yes! I don't know how, but I can use magic in real life!"

"Like hell you can!"

Kokone was even more elated at confirming she could use magic. Morio, in contrast, remained skeptical.

"I'll admit, these things that keep happening to us do seem magical, but it's gotta be some kind of trick." Morio turned to the vendor. "…Who paid for these?"

She replied with nothing but her beautiful, professional smile and pushed her cart onward.

Maybe our benefactor told her not to say anything? It could be. No, there's no doubt. Unsatisfied, Morio stared at the bento boxes. Kokone had already begun to dig in.

"You gonna eat, Morio?" she asked, grinning ear to ear. She picked up the tablet lying next to her and wrote her father another message:

"The bento came! We're heading to Tokyo on the bullet train."

As Kokone tapped ENTER, she looked like a girl getting ready to go on a field trip.

"They're on a bullet train?! I thought they didn't have any money."

"That's what I thought."

Officer Koyama was the one who found Kokone's messages on the social networking app. Watanabe had called him after leaving the Morikawa home, searching for clues on her location.

In accordance with Watanabe's instructions, Officer Koyama had sent the messages *"Where are you?"* and *"Stay there"*, but despite his efforts, Kokone was nearing Shijima's headquarters in Tokyo.

I have no choice but to get to headquarters first and stop them myself..., Watanabe thought.

"Tell me if she writes anything else," he said to Officer Koyama as he walked up the ramp to the company's private jet.

"...I hope you aren't mistaking the police for your personal henchmen," Officer Koyama crossly replied.

"Hmm? We pay our taxes, and if anything, we're assisting in the investigation. What are you complaining about, exactly?" Watanabe retorted before hanging up and telling the pilot to head to Haneda Airport.

Officer Koyama folded his cell phone and shoved it into his pocket. *Who does he think he is?* Officer Tsukamoto handed his seething colleague a cup of vending machine coffee.

The pair analyzed the facts of the Momotarou Morikawa / Shijima Motors case over their drinks. Momotarou Morikawa had graduated from a technical high school in Okayama and immediately moved to Tokyo to serve as a contractor at Shijima Technical Research Facility, a division of Shijima Motors.

Around that time, he had happened to meet Ikumi Shijima, Chairman Shijima's daughter, and the two had married in no time.

It was a well-kept secret how a mere contractor came to wed the next president of Shijima Motors. Ikumi's relationship with her father had already been strained, and her marriage hadn't been covered by the media. Only a select few knew of it at all.

Ikumi and Momotarou's married life had lasted only a year, until Ikumi had perished in an accident. Soon after the event, Momotarou had returned to Okayama with the infant Kokone.

Though Ikumi's death had been purely an accident, not many knew the couple had had a child, which meant Kokone's birth had not been cause for celebration among Shijima's upper echelon despite her Shijima blood, or so the officers reasoned.

But why had Momotarou Morikawa suddenly stolen Shijima Motors' data after almost eighteen peaceful years in the countryside? Watanabe had said that Momotarou had likely needed a large sum of money to pay for his daughter's college education. But based on the expenditure and income records they had obtained, the Morikawas didn't seem particularly strapped for cash, and Kokone had an educational endowment insurance plan.

After a second review of Momotarou's motives, Koyama couldn't stand it anymore and voiced his doubts. "Do you think Morikawa really stole the data?"

Tsukamoto had the same misgivings and grunted in agreement. "…There's not much we can do as long as he refuses to talk to us."

"…Right."

Ever since the officers had taken his phone, Momotarou had refused to say another word, as though he was steadfastly guarding something from them. Based on his records, Momotarou's life had suggested he was honest, if awkward, and something about him told Tsukamoto, who had seen many criminals in his time, that this man was innocent.

Morio was unable to suppress his hunger as he watched Kokone voraciously wolfing down her bento box, and he opened his own.

Once he had eaten about half of it and calmed down a little, he took his AR goggles from his bag and put them on. He had only surface-level knowledge of Shijima Motors and its chairman, Isshin Shijima, so he wanted to dig deeper.

"…This is Mom's father…?"

"Yup."

After syncing Kokone's tablet so she could see the search results as well, Morio typed on the virtual keyboard. He had seen Isshin

Shijima's face only a few times, on the news, so he remembered it vaguely. Kokone, on the other hand, hadn't even known Shijima Motors existed.

"Isshin Shijima is the founder and current chairman of the Japanese automobile manufacturer Shijima Motors," Morio read from the Shijima Motors Wikipedia page. It was unclear how much Kokone had heard—she was busy intensely peering at Isshin Shijima's photos. In every picture, Isshin's expression was severe, and he projected an aura of unapproachability.

"He looks so scary. I'm not a fan of having him as my grandpa...," commented Kokone. But her scrolling stopped when she reached one particular photo. It was from an auto show twenty years ago—Isshin was being mobbed by microphones and tape recorders, and behind him, a lonely-looking Ikumi Shijima was staring at some documents.

"Your mom graduated from Carnegie Mellon in the United States and immediately became an employee of the company... But a year before her death, she left Shijima Motors because of a falling-out with her father, the chairman."

They did another image search but found nothing for Ikumi Shijima other than the picture Kokone had already found. Kokone gave up on finding more images of her mother and asked Morio the next question that naturally came to her mind.

"What about Dad?"

Morio sifted through all the information on Wikipedia, even the claims marked *citation needed*, but found nothing on a Momotarou.

"Nothing. Which means this 'falling-out' must have been your mother's marriage to Uncle Momo."

"Huh..." Kokone made a sound of slight disappointment and went back to looking at Ikumi's photo.

The only daughter of the founder of one of Japan's greatest companies. A genius who had established herself as its successor at a young age immediately after graduating from one of the top universities in the United States.

"Mom was an amazing person…"

Even Kokone had to take a step back in awe of her mother, who had lived in a completely different world, Morio noticed.

"My dad's amazing, too, isn't he? I mean, he married her."

Or maybe he had thought too much. Kokone wasn't so much taking a step back as she was hurtling toward her.

"Well, yeah, I…guess."

Ugh, eternally positive, aren't you…? Morio honestly admired her.

"I wonder how Mom and Dad met and ended up marrying?" Kokone's thoughts turned toward her parents' romance. "Morio, look up where Shijima Motors is, would you?"

"Huh?"

Morio lifted his AR goggles up and stared at Kokone, who had been lost in a fantasy about the romance between her parents not a moment ago. As if called by some unseen force, she descended into the world of her dreams.

*   *   *

Heartland was covered in a thick blanket of fog just before dawn.

In the middle of it stood Ancien and Peach. They had avoided Bewan's ambush thanks to Heart's heroics and returned to Heartland from Hill Mountain to fulfill their objective. The roads were usually congested twenty-four hours a day, but there were no cars now, perhaps due to the kingdom-wide curfew imposed because of the demon's repeated onslaughts.

After observing Heartland Castle from a good vantage point with her binoculars, Ancien asked Peach to drive Heart at the Engine Heads who stood guarding the castle gates.

"Toward that one!"

With a grunt of affirmation, Peach revved the engine loudly and hurtled in the direction of one of the machines.

Hidden in the fog, Heart ran through the downtown area. The streets were littered with rubble from the buildings destroyed by the demon. Ancien sorrowfully took in the sight.

This wouldn't have happened if she had completed the spell of Spirit earlier.

Regret welled up in her throat, but she managed to swallow it and face forward again.

Ancien and Peach sneaked through the thinly patrolled streets. Once they had made it to the Engine Head's feet, they left Heart and climbed the ladder left next to the machine, intending to make it inside.

The Engine Heads' interiors had control rooms for each body part, connected by passageways that ran every which way. Ancien opened the entry hatch and infiltrated the duct-like corridors. With Joy on her shoulder and Peach behind her, she made her way forward on all fours. Finally, they reached a ladder running perpendicular to their path, and above, they could hear the voices of men.

They had found the Engine Head's bridge.

Ancien and Joy climbed the ladder and peered into the bridge from the entrance. They could see the captain's back between two consoles. A large window stood before him, and Heartland's Gulf Area was visible beyond it. In front of the window were several control panels, and multiple pilots sat ready to launch, peering keenly at the view outside. Thanks to that, not a single person was looking back.

Seizing the opportunity, Ancien scanned the bridge and found what she was looking for—a switchboard connected to the Engine Head's main computer.

"Now's our chance!" Ancien signaled Peach, and they crawled into the bridge on their forearms. They opened the switchboard's panel, disconnected the cables, and attached the magic tablet to it.

Joy had leaped from Ancien's shoulder and was gazing at her to spur her on. Peach put his hand on Ancien's shoulder to give her courage.

The two had returned to Heartland to download the completed Spirit spell into the Engine Head and defeat the demon.

"Captain! The demon has appeared!" a pilot yelled, and a thrill of anxiety washed over the bridge.

Peach kept his hand on Ancien's shoulder and glanced sharply toward the source of the voice.

"It seems so." The captain was acting calm, but he was trembling in fear on the inside. This creature's might had already felled one of the kingdom's three Engine Heads.

Peach rose slightly and looked out the window to see the demon making a beeline for the other Engine Head a distance away. The sinister black giant began forcing the Engine Head to the ground—clearly, they were struggling.

"Captain, shouldn't we assist Unit Two?" asked a steersman.

The captain's anger surfaced as he yelled, "O-our mission is to protect this gate with our lives! We must not move from this spot!"

Peach realized the captain's fear was making him want to run away. He couldn't help but wonder aloud, "When are you going to fight that demon if not now?"

The country was filled with people who had stopped thinking independently and simply followed the king's orders. Peach turned back to Ancien and urged her to use her magic to shine a ray of light into a land frozen in its old ways.

"This is a chance for the king to accept the power of magic."

"Yeah!" Ancien typed the spell of Spirit into the tablet. "'With spirit alone, we can soar. Mechanical giant, combat the demon with your own will!' Send!"

The tablet suddenly started overflowing with light. The same light spilled from the instruments on the bridge, and luminous threads ran between them as if creating a new network. The pilots all shouted in surprise, but before they had a moment to react, the light was coursing through the entire Engine Head.

The enormous machine, shrouded with a magical glow, took a step without anybody moving it.

"Hey, what's going on? Why did its leg just move?" the captain cried out, shocked that the Engine Head was advancing independent of his orders.

With each step, the giant's movements became smoother and more rapid. It ran toward the demon, faster and faster, as if unable to contain its joy at being able to walk and run of its own volition.

Ancien, Peach, and Joy looked at one another.

"Well done, Ancien."

"Yeah!"

The captain's face was getting whiter with every word. "Hey, stop it! Stop moving on your own!"

For him, it was more important not to make a mistake than to fight the demon. He grabbed the microphone and yelled into it in desperation. "Both legs! Pull the brakes!"

Hearing this, Ancien leaped up from behind the console where she was hiding. "You can't!"

The captain spun around.

"It's fighting with its own will. This battle belongs to it!"

"Who are you?!"

"It's a magic user!"

Not only the captain but the entire crew turned toward Ancien.

The captain flushed bright red with embarrassment, convinced Ancien had ruined his image. "Where did you come from?! Throw them out!"

Joy came to her rescue. "Such insolence! Ancien is a princess!"

The crew briefly hesitated but decided to charge Ancien and pin her down. Ancien swiftly dodged their bodies and put the tablet in her bag, but Joy was hurled aside in the process. Peach jumped out in Joy's stead.

"Don't get in our way!" Peach grappled with the pilots and flung them across the room as they came, one by one, unflinching even when they punched him.

This wouldn't end well. Still red-faced, the captain screamed hysterically. "All divisions, stop this crazy thing!"

Despite their confusion, the steersmen in the arm and leg stations slammed on the brakes as the intercom had ordered.

"Graaaaaaagh!" The steersmen desperately gritted their teeth, and the brakes, not designed for this sort of load, screeched and began to smoke. Sweat poured down the men's foreheads.

But the Engine Head wouldn't stop. Sprinting through the town, it let the momentum carry it toward the demon and raised its right arm to take it down.

The captain saw no choice but to use his last resort.

"Kill the engine!" he shrieked into the microphone.

Before the captain could finish his order, the Engine Head's right arm came down on the demon with tremendous force and a speed that far surpassed anything the crew had managed.

With one blow, the demon's head was split in two, and a red, lava-like substance flowed from the wound. The demon dropped to its knees, and the Engine Head raised his arm once more with the intent to deliver a finishing blow.

Just then, the Engine Head's engine plugs shot out from the deck in its head with a loud bang. Black smoke poured from the holes where the plugs had been, and the machine went still. The chief engineer had purged the engine plugs as per the captain's orders. The Engine Head, though powered by magic, could do nothing with its engine shut off.

The captain grunted happily, even though he'd missed the chance to defeat the demon with just one more hit.

"Good job, crew! We will defend our post with our lives."

What he intended to protect with an inoperative machine was unclear.

Ancien, unable to contain her anger, jumped to her feet.

Peach had been watching the events unfold as his scuffle with the crew continued, and he called out to her. "Ancien, don't give up!"

She turned to him. He was right—they couldn't give up now.

"Go to the deck and replace the plugs manually!" Of course—Peach was a mechanical expert.

Ancien nodded to show she understood and, weaving through the crew members' arms, opened the bridge's window. A strong gust of wind swept in and blew away Ancien's hat. Undeterred, she leaped out the window.

But the Engine Head's deck was almost five hundred feet from the ground, high enough to make anybody dizzy. Ancien grabbed on to the ladder for dear life and began her climb toward the head.

A powerful wind violently tugged at Ancien's skirt, and she clutched at the ladder as she lost her balance. She looked down and saw the crouching demon, its head still split open. But lava continued to pour from its wound. It flowed over the injury as the demon attempted to heal itself.

"The demon's gonna come back..." Ancien climbed the ladder with renewed resolve.

A girl watched this occur from a faraway building—Kokone, as she appeared in real life.

"Go, Ancien!" she whispered, before she sensed something strange. "Wait, I'm in my dream as myself?"

Ordinarily, Kokone would have appeared as Ancien.

*   *   *

Ancien made it up the ladder and arrived at the deck. The Engine Head had frozen on a tilt, so the deck was also lopsided. There were no handrails or grips—the only objects protruding from the flat deck were the six engine plugs. They were huge up close—each one was more than thirty feet long.

Ancien made a dash for the plug closest to her. The exposed portion of each plug was grooved, like a screw. If she pulled the emergency lever above each one, the plug would twist itself back into the machine, and the engine would run once more. Ancien jumped up to grab the lever, which was high over her head, and pulled with all her weight. The handle came down, and the plug made a sound. Ancien let go and dropped to the deck before making her way to the next one. Behind her, the plug she had just activated was rotating into its hole.

"Yes!"

She pulled the next one with her body weight, then moved on to the next.

Meanwhile, down at the bridge, Peach had taken down the crew members attempting to chase after Ancien and was now leaping out the window. Kicking the crew members back into their cockpit, Peach started up the ladder toward Ancien. Joy clung onto his back. They were not intimidated by the five-hundred-foot height—they had decided to protect Ancien no matter what.

But the crew would not pursue them farther. No matter what the captain's orders were, their fear prevented them from stepping outside.

Kokone, who had slipped into the dream, saw that the demon at the Engine Head's feet was reforming its lava into an arm and reaching out for the mechanical giant.

"What should I do?"

Instinctively, Kokone started running toward the Engine Head.

Ancien had not noticed the demon's actions, and she continued to pull the levers. Just one more. Once she triggered the last one, the Engine Head would roar back to life and deliver a final blow to the demon. The machine's victory—and the moment that Ancien's magic would be of use to Heartland—was moments away.

By the time Peach reached the deck, Ancien had started toward the final plug. Peach waved his hand, and Ancien waved back with a smile. She sprang onto the final lever.

But at that moment, the demon's new arm grabbed the Engine Head's leg. The tilted structure further lost its balance.

"Aahh!" Ancien gripped the lever, swinging wildly back and forth as the great machine shuddered.

Peach, too, was left dangling on the ladder by one hand.

Kokone gulped, dashing through her dream world.

"Yikes, I've gotta help them."

But no matter how hard she ran, her body refused to advance. Kokone looked up to check how Ancien and Peach were doing. Just then, a sense of déjà vu washed over her.

"Hmm? …Hey, I feel like this was the end of the fairy tale Dad told us…"

Clinging to Peach's neck, Joy could see that Ancien was swinging her body on the lever, trying to yank it down. If the plug were to fall into place, there wouldn't be anything for her to grab on to. Determined, Ancien threw her weight onto the lever, pulled it all the way down, and then let go. She slid down the steeply angled deck at a dangerous speed toward Peach. He would catch her, she knew, and she trusted her life to him.

"Ancien!"

Ancien pulled her tablet from her bag as she slid and jumped toward the voice.

Hanging from the deck with his left hand, Peach stretched out his right and grabbed the edge of the tablet in Ancien's hands.

"We did it!"

Ancien dangled with both hands from the tablet, which Peach still clutched. Joy inched down Peach's right arm in an attempt to help the girl. Joy's short arms were just shy of reaching her hands, but Ancien's fingers lost their grip and slipped down the tablet, managing to regain their hold at its very edge. Peach was supporting both his and Ancien's weights with one arm, and he was nearly at his limit.

"Guh…!" Peach poured the last of his strength into his right arm to try to pull Ancien up. At that moment, the tablet's screen cracked under the pressure.

At this rate, the magic tablet, Ancien, Peach, and Joy would all be lost.

"Peach…"

As Peach ground his teeth together in his attempt to pull Ancien up, a soft voice called to him.

Peach looked down with a gasp. Hanging from the tablet where Ancien had been was now Ikumi.

Kokone could see what Peach saw from where she stood. The mother she saw was not the one from the portrait back home, but the one she had seen on the Internet—the lonely-looking Ikumi.

Ikumi looked Peach and Joy in the eye and smiled warmly.

"Peach, I'm sorry…I couldn't stay with you until the end. But I'll come back whenever you need me. Take care of Kokone until then."

Peach understood everything from her tone of voice—she meant to fall from the tablet to save him and Joy.

Ikumi let go.

Pride in herself for having tried to protect Heartland, sadness at not having been able to watch over Kokone's growth, happiness at having entrusted everything to Peach... With all these feelings in her heart, Ikumi slowly fell.

*　*　*

"Mom...why...?"

Kokone bolted upright when she awoke from her dream. They were still on the bullet train. Tears welled in her open eyes and rolled down her face. Without even wiping them away, Kokone reflected on her dream and what she had realized.

"I'd always thought...I was that story's main character..."

A long-forgotten memory reemerged in Kokone's mind—a time when Momotarou had been so close by Kokone's side that she had hardly realized she didn't have a mother.

"Wake up! Daddy, stop sleeping." After a long day of work and child-rearing, Momotarou often passed out in the living room until Kokone shook him awake.

Even then, Momotarou had always been willing to be Kokone's playmate. He had tossed her up in the air and given her spare engine parts to play with. Kokone had taken to thinking of the engine in the workshop as a castle, lining up cylinders in front of it and pretending they were robots guarding the castle. Model cars, too. Momotarou gave them all to her.

Kokone, now a paragon of health, had often had fevers when she was little. As she lay with Joy on her mattress, Momotarou would always come by with his tablet after work. He had called the cracked device his magic tablet.

Momotarou had typed "spells" into the tablet using simple characters for Kokone's benefit.

"With spirit alone, your fever will go away."

The belief that her father could cure her fever with magic had been more effective than any medicine. Kokone had read the tablet's spell with him.

"With spirit...alone, your...fever will go...away."

Momotarou would hold Kokone's hand and press it to the ENTER button.

"Enter!" they said together.

Joy was always with her, fever or not. It was next to her when she went to sleep and was the first one Kokone greeted upon waking. It was her best friend, who had seen her at her happiest and saddest. All because of her father, who had given her mother's precious Joy to her. It had seen her mother through her highs and lows, as well.

"What's wrong? Can't sleep?"

Momotarou had told her the story of "Ancien and the Magic Tablet" on restless nights. The story of Peach and Ancien's first encounter. Their quest to slay the demon. Their various encounters with the many little people of the kingdom and subsequent friendships. The magic spells they thought up to give life to their friends and the Engine Head. How they left the kingdom with their magic tablet and settled in Hill Mountain...

"And this is that tablet."

When Momotarou told these stories, he seemed proud and happy but also lonely. After the elopement and Ikumi's death, Momotarou had cut all ties with Shijima. But he had told Kokone what an intelligent, honest, wonderful woman Ikumi was through his stories, hoping his daughter would grow up to be the same. It was thanks to these stories about Ikumi that Kokone was able to sleep easy those nights.

It had been right there the entire time, all around her. She hadn't even really thought about these things, because she took them for granted. At long last, it all made sense to her and came together within Kokone.

"…Dad. I always wondered why you never told me anything about Mom…" She drew a shuddery breath in and let it out slowly. Her lips trembled. "But you were always telling me so, so much about her."

Kokone wiped away the overflowing tears and faced forward. Morio was going back and forth, unsure of what to say to her after she had immediately started crying once she woke up.

"…Morio, where are we?" she asked.

The bullet train had left Shinagawa and was on its way to Tokyo Station.

Chapter 4

Seeing the Tokyo Tower from the train's window, Kokone truly felt they had at last arrived in Tokyo. She had only ever seen the metropolis on television. She had never seen buildings so tall back at home, and they were racing past her one after the next.

Just a little longer, and they would be at Shijima Motors and find her grandfather, the man who had misunderstood her dad and disowned her mom.

After disembarking from the train, the two did a search on Morio's phone for another train they could take to Shijima Headquarters. It was in an area facing Tokyo Bay, and it would take 460 yen and one transfer to get to the nearest station, Daiba. It would take 920 yen for the two to get there, not to mention the ride back. Morio and Kokone searched their wallets. Even with Kokone's 650 yen, it wasn't enough.

"You could get there if you went alone. Do you feel like trying the magic tablet again?"

Kokone *hmm*ed at Morio's suggestion. Then, for the third time, a stranger called out to them.

"Are you Kokone Morikawa?"

Kokone lifted her face and saw a middle-aged man with round glasses smiling awkwardly at her, wringing his hands. At his sides were a fat man and a pallid man. Kokone didn't recognize any of them, but they wore the same clothes as the pair from the gas station in Osaka.

"A-are they with that bearded guy?!"

Morio instinctively raised his hands and put himself in between Kokone and the men. He had no confidence in his physical prowess, but he summoned his courage and called, "Kokone, go! I'll take care of this!"

"Uh, but…"

Kokone was unsure, but Morio had decided that without the money for a train ticket, all he could do was hold off these men.

"It'll be okay! You have the tablet!"

"But what'll you do, Morio?"

Though she was grateful, Kokone saw reason to be far more concerned about Morio's sudden theatrics. At the same time, she did have priorities…

Perhaps sensing Kokone's conflict—or perhaps not—Morio made another dramatic declaration before the enemy could regain their lost ground.

"Don't worry about me, Kokone, and run!" He charged at the three, not believing for a second that he would win.

"Whoa! You've got us all wrong!" The man with glasses backed away and raised his arms to shield himself.

"All wrong my ass!" Morio said, eyes closed and fists swinging.

"Um…," the man began apologetically, and Morio heard the sincerity in his voice. He stopped, looked up, and followed the man's finger pointing behind him. Kokone was no longer there, speeding down the stairs at the far end of the station.

"…What?! I'm being so brave, and she's not even watching?"

Morio's confidence crumbled. Still, he had managed to intimidate the men into stopping their pursuit of Kokone, and he desperately grabbed at the one with glasses. Although at this point, it was more an act to preserve his dignity than anything else.

As Morio squeezed his neck, the spectacled man rasped, "Um… would you mind listening to us?"

"Shut it!"

The two other men gave up on pursuing Kokone and started pulling Morio away from their friend.

"We've come here to save Mr. Momotarou," the spectacled man choked out.

"What?!" Morio's arms relaxed for a second, and the two men took the chance to seize him by the armpits. "But you're from Shijima Motors, aren't you?"

As Morio's hostility showed no sign of abating, the spectacled man took his phone from his pocket and showed him its home screen. The man's phone had an app marked with a skull on it, the same as Momotarou's tablet.

"That icon…"

"That's right. It's for the application Ancient Heart, the app we created with Momotarou for automobile enthusiasts everywhere to secretly communicate!"

Morio saw the timeline and finally understood. "I see. You've been reading the messages Kokone wrote on the app."

Morio still didn't completely trust them, but now that he knew these men were responsible for the miracle in Osaka, he felt his blood cooling.

"Yes, we have. Thanks to those messages, we were able to beat Watanabe to the punch and ready the bullet-train tickets and bento boxes for you."

Morio had now learned the trick behind the "magic," albeit from an unexpected source, but he still had many questions. Why were different people, all from Shijima Motors, variously trying to steal the tablet and keep it safe?

"But doesn't Shijima Motors want the tablet?"

The spectacled man nodded at the straightforward question. "That's true, but Ms. Ikumi left an impact on those of us in the resistance. We don't want Watanabe to have what's on it."

This group calling themselves "the resistance" belonged to the Shijima Technical Research Group, and they mainly performed electrical work.

"We used to work with Mr. Momotarou…," the man started, beginning his story.

Back then, the most important parts of automobile manufacturing were said to be engine design, development, the chassis design, and overall design. Engineers who worked with electronics and other materials were treated as if they were a rung lower on the ladder, even though they were working on the same cars.

But in recent years, due to the universality of the Internet, the automobile industry reached a point where it could not go without integrating information technology into its designs. Ikumi Shijima, who had foreseen this twenty years earlier, had advocated the view that their company should free itself of the shackles of the past and begin incorporating IT. But her views clashed with her father's, and she was thrown out of the company's main branch.

Ikumi had chosen to entrust her ideas to the Shijima Technical Research Group, which had handled all of Shijima Motors' electrical work.

The man in glasses recounted his story keenly, as though meditating on the time gone by.

"To this day, we still admire Ms. Ikumi for entrusting her intelligence to mere workers like us. And we still revere Momotarou Morikawa as a legend of engineering and the man she opened her heart to. We keep in contact with him to this day, and that's why we're here to help you in his time of need."

"And you used the app…?"

"Yes… But after his treatment at Shijima's hands, it seems Momotarou isn't too fond of us," the man in glasses said self-deprecatingly, looking down.

"Not much we can do about that. Anybody would feel that way after Shijima legally cut all ties with them," the fat man added. "Right after Mr. Momotarou and Ms. Ikumi got married, Watanabe made them promise never to claim the right to anything against Shijima. He was Shijima's lawyer at the time."

"He always looked down on people working in our field. Nobody liked him. And he's the director of the company now, so as you can imagine, we're not really motivated to work," continued the pallid man.

Now that he understood how things had gotten to this point, Morio opened his mouth to speak. "Then what does the tablet contain? Why would someone with Watanabe's status risk so much to get his hands on it?"

"The tablet contains Ikumi's original code for self-driving cars."

"Huh…" Hearing this, Morio realized how Momotarou's self-driving vehicles could be considered magic. Morio had been considering the possibility as an explanation ever since he'd read Ikumi's profile on the bullet train, but this had confirmed it. "I see now. Uncle Momo had the magic spell from the start," he muttered.

"That's right," the man in glasses said. "But Mr. Momotarou was the one who used the program to create an actual self-driving vehicle. It's an admirable feat."

"Not even those of us at Shijima Motors have managed to create a stand-alone self-driving car," commented the fat man.

Morio was reminded of the company's plan to have the athletes ride self-driving cars at the Tokyo Olympics opening ceremony.

"So does that mean…?"

"Yes. The self-driving cars for the Olympics aren't finished. That's why Watanabe needs Mr. Momotarou's tablet."

All the pieces had finally come together. He understood why Momotarou had suddenly been arrested, how he must have felt in custody…

"Let's go save Uncle Momo!"

Morio enthusiastically invited the men in work clothes to join forces with him.

Kokone had managed to transfer to the Yurikamome Line and was on her way to Daiba. She had never ridden a train this smooth in her life, and the sheer number of people around her was overwhelming. The Rainbow Bridge outside the window drew her gaze. She thought of the Great Seto Bridge back at home and imagined it superimposed on the bridge her mother had seen all those years ago, although the images didn't line up.

The train arrived at Daiba Station in no time.

Luckily, Shijima Motors' headquarters was right by the station, and Kokone made it there without getting lost. She walked into the lobby of the giant building with an enormous *S* logo affixed high on its side.

The lobby's ceiling was open to the top floor. Banners hung in the air, the same five colors as the Olympic rings. The lobby functioned as a showcase for famous cars manufactured by Shijima Motors, as well as shiny concept vehicles.

Perhaps because it was the first day of summer vacation before the Olympics, the lobby was full of television crews holding cameras, mass media personnel, and families with children. A little boy sat on his father's shoulders, pointing at the open ceiling. Kokone looked to see what had caught his interest. A balloon of the Shijima Motors mascot and its giant wings floated above, and from its neck hung a banner announcing Shijima Motors as an official sponsor of the Tokyo Olympics.

They mentioned that on the news yesterday morning, Kokone remembered languidly. Back then, she never would have thought she'd be in Tokyo now.

"…?!"

Kokone's eyes were drawn to the motto written on the top of the banner.

With Spirit Alone, We Can Soar.

The same words were written on the metal sheet at Morikawa Motors' workshop.

"That's the same motto as ours…"

"Idiot! Where's your nerve?!"

Isshin Shijima's angry shouts resounded through the chairman's office.

Several direct subordinates of the president had come into the room to give instructions to the chairman in person. They stood around his desk, their heads hanging.

The issue was with the self-driving cars scheduled to be released at the Olympics two days from now. Now, of all times, the president's employees had expressed their opposition to the idea of putting the athletes in autonomous vehicles at the opening ceremony, concerned that they could not risk failure in front of the whole world at the Olympics.

According to the chairman's representatives, if Shijima Motors could unveil the world's first self-driving cars at the Olympics, the company's impact on the world would be immeasurable. According to him, this was the best chance for the company, which was currently on a downhill slide at the mercy of its competitors' prices and technological advancements, to once again become "the world-famous Shijima."

He had personally convinced the workers who wanted more than anything to take safety precautions and encouraged engineers to put all their efforts into the project.

Seeing the chairman's intense and almost possessed passion, the old guard had felt an uneasiness. Their "downhill slide" had started when Isshin had stepped down as president and installed himself as chairman, and their next-in-line, Ikumi, had left the company. Their anxiety was related to how the chairman had personally opposed the production of self-driving cars when Ikumi had proposed it almost twenty years ago.

"But the Olympics are only two days away. If a car carrying an athlete were to have an accident, Shijima wouldn't just be embarrassed. The mass media are already reporting this might happen... We need to allow drivers in the cars!"

Chairman Shijima's expression did not change in the slightest at the president's objections. He stared out the window and declared:

"No. We will conduct the opening ceremony with self-driving cars."

Though he was now only the chairman, Isshin Shijima was still the man who had built this company from the ground up. The men stood there lifelessly, wondering whether their company was destined to fail because this old man wanted to atone for his behavior toward his late daughter.

"...I've made up my mind. Stop wasting time!"

Chairman Shijima continued staring out the window, not even bothering to turn back to the president and his employees.

After he left the chairman's office, the president was too irritated to go back to his own room. Instead, he went to the lobby and called Watanabe, who had returned to Haneda Airport by private jet and should have been on his way back to Shijima Headquarters.

It was only two weeks ago that Watanabe had told him how Ikumi had completed the program for self-driving cars twenty years ago.

The people of Shijima Motors had believed that Ikumi's death in an accident while testing a self-driving car had been due to a flaw in the programming. In truth, the cause had been a collision brought about by an unrelated automobile, but Shijima Motors had chosen to pin the accident on Momotarou Morikawa, her coinventor.

Watanabe, who had overseen the legal aftermath of the accident back then, had ordered Momotarou to relinquish his rights, saying that in return, Shijima Motors wouldn't press charges. But Momotarou had told him he would never hand over his daughter, Kokone, nor Ikumi's original code. Watanabe, distracted by the idea that Ikumi's child might eventually become Shijima's heir, had agreed to let Momotarou have the original code.

But when the flaws in the self-driving car for the Olympics had become apparent, Watanabe, who had heard rumors that Momotarou had perfected the technology, remembered the existence of Ikumi's original code and decided to take it for himself.

They would get their hands on the code and complete the self-driving car in time for the Olympics, unbeknownst to the chairman. That was how Watanabe and his followers planned to protect Shijima Motors' image while ousting the chairman and taking his place.

Watanabe answered the phone.

"Well?" the president asked impatiently. "Have you obtained the original code?"

"Soon."

"Don't be so reckless. You're being too obvious."

It was one thing to use Shijima Motors' private jet, but involving the police was a dangerous gamble. It increased the chances of the media catching on.

But Watanabe simply laughed and brushed him off. "Can't afford to play it safe. If our demonstration at the Olympics doesn't go well, we'll be affected, too. Some risk is unavoidable. We'll just have to take care of the rest with money."

"But…"

"The chairman is repenting for his misdeeds toward his late daughter; he isn't interested in the future of autonomous vehicles. After the Olympics, we'll get rid of him on those grounds. Out with the old and in with the new, which is us." Watanabe laughed unapologetically. "But first and foremost, we need the Olympics to go well."

In truth, Watanabe was even more concerned than the president.

I won't let that bumpkin girl ruin my future!

Watanabe had become so irrational that he remained totally unaware of how his actions were turning him into a villain in a low-budget television drama.

WITH SPIRIT ALONE, WE CAN SOAR—Kokone stared at the banner for a while, but then she remembered why she had come here, and she headed to the lobby's reception desk. Three women sat at the desk, looking exactly like the epitome of receptionists for a large corporation. Kokone found them difficult to approach. She felt she would immediately betray her country upbringing. Kokone chose the happiest looking of the women and tried speaking to her.

"Um, I would like to meet with Chairman Shijima, please," said Kokone, being careful not to let her accent slip in.

The receptionist observed Kokone's face, then looked her over all the way down to her fingertips before returning her gaze to Kokone's face.

Bleached brown hair, and those short skirts all the high schoolers are wearing these days—who is this yokel?

Fully masking her thoughts, the receptionist smiled at Kokone. "And for what purpose?"

"I'm Chairman Shijima's granddaughter. I'm here about my father…" Kokone took an honest approach, partially because she couldn't think of anything better.

The receptionist couldn't help but react to Kokone's bold assertion.

She knit her brows and, lowering her voice, replied condescendingly, "...That isn't very funny. The chairman's daughter passed away long ago."

"I know, but..." Though Kokone had not uttered a single lie earlier, she didn't know how she might better explain the circumstances. She searched frantically for something else to say, but finally, she opted for "I'm sorry, I'll be back" and left the lobby.

Another receptionist, overhearing their conversation, glanced at Kokone to see which way she was going. She then whipped out her phone and tapped its screen. A skull icon, the same one the resistance used, was on its menu.

Kokone left the headquarters' air-conditioned lobby. She had no particular course of action in mind and stood there wondering what to do next. But soon, the asphalt underneath her feet started getting uncomfortably hot, and Kokone, unable to stand it, walked toward the promenade at the back of the building in search of somewhere cool to think.

She encountered a vending machine on the way and checked her funds. Having spent 460 yen for the train, she now had 190.

"Hmm..."

If she bought a drink here, she would have only 40 yen left. But she wouldn't be able to return to Tokyo Station with only 190 yen anyhow. Deciding to soothe her dry throat for the time being, she bought a bottle of tea. She pressed the cold plastic to her cheek and sat in the shade.

She had fully planned out what she wanted to say to Chairman Shijima, but she hadn't anticipated being turned away at the reception desk. Kokone looked up at the headquarters.

My grandfather's in there. Maybe I'll get to see him if I just walk in anyway? If worse came to worst, she could force her way past... Kokone repositioned the bottle of tea to open it.

An old man in a suit walked past her, and her eyes subconsciously followed him. The dots didn't connect immediately, but she realized after a moment that he might be the same person from the photo she'd seen on the bullet train.

"That man…?!"

Kokone hurriedly chased after him.

After Isshin had dismissed the president from his office, he had stared out his window until his secretary, one of the only people he trusted, had called out to him.

"You seem awfully tired. May I suggest a walk in the garden?" It was an unusual suggestion.

The garden? Now? A protest had crossed his mind, but the idea had appealed to Isshin's troubled soul.

"Twenty minutes, just until my next appointment," he'd said, leaving the room. As he did, he had looked up at the motto affixed over the entrance of his office.

WITH SPIRIT ALONE, WE CAN SOAR.

Seeing that the chairman had left the room, the secretary took out her phone. The skull icon was there, too.

The garden behind Shijima Headquarters was slightly elevated, offering a view of the sea. The Rainbow Bridge, too, was visible from the tip of the cape surrounded by green hedges. The water's surface glittered in the sun, and the ocean breeze blew pleasantly past the promontory.

The man Kokone was following stood at the overlook and gazed out at the far-off horizon. *Gazing* was perhaps not the right word—the man was glaring. His aura made that much clear, even from behind. A force poured from his being that discouraged other people from approaching.

Everything Kokone had prepared to say left her, and she ended up speaking to the man without a plan at all.

"Um…," she said in a voice so timid she could barely believe it was hers.

Isshin turned slowly toward her, irritation at the disturbance written on his face.

"What?" he snapped, his brow furrowed.

"Er… Would you like some tea?" Kokone forced a smile and handed him the bottle.

I'm so glad I didn't open it. She would lose this fight if she allowed herself to be overwhelmed. Kokone summoned her usual casual attitude and clenched her stomach. *I'm not gonna be weird!*

When a girl far younger than he struck up a conversation, Isshin was surprised, yet he felt his guard relaxing.

"Alone on such a fair day?" he asked.

"Yeah. I was going to meet with someone, but I couldn't. I was wondering what I should do…here."

Kokone gave up the idea that he might recognize her and decided not to reveal her identity to the stubborn Isshin until later. She figured she would have an easier time acting normal that way, too.

Kokone indicated the bench behind her with a glance. Isshin sat down, and Kokone set her things on the ground and took a seat next to him about a person's width away.

"So? Were you planning to keep wasting your time doing that?" asked Isshin, looking out at the sea. Nothing about his behavior suggested he had any intention of having a proper conversation with Kokone.

"Huh?"

"I'd advise you to choose your next course of action soon. Life may seem long, but it's actually quite brief." Isshin glanced at her, then closed his mouth as if to end the conversation.

"Oh really? Life is short, huh…?" Kokone replied, undeterred. She wouldn't get a second chance if this conversation were to end.

"Sadly."

Isshin seemed ready to stand up at any moment, but Kokone held him back with another question.

"When did you start thinking that?"

"Hmm…?"

Her question struck a chord with Isshin. Most people these days talked only about themselves, even at work, and ignored not only what others said but also their questions. Yet this girl was boldly asking about the thoughts of an older man.

He looked directly at Kokone for the first time. She had an aura of wonder and pureness that made Isshin reluctant to label her a mere delinquent. And a familiar plushie protruded from the burlap sack in her lap.

"For me, life still feels so *long*, you know?"

As the inquisitive girl leaned forward, Isshin found it oddly difficult to meet her eyes, and he looked away. Recalling why he had told this stranger that life is short, he replied:

"I wonder… It might have been when my rebellious daughter passed on to heaven at such a young age…"

Isshin wondered whether Ikumi had thought her life long or short. As for himself, his life had ended when Ikumi was an infant who would not have survived but for his support. His time on this earth had meaning not when he was working or having fun, but when somebody had needed him. That had been the only thought in his mind back when he learned of Ikumi's death.

Kokone stared at Isshin's face as he gazed into the distance as though in remembrance of somebody. She was thinking of someone, herself.

The ocean breeze blew through her hair, as if that very someone were urging her on.

"…What kind of person was she?"

How was this girl managing to strike right to the heart of the mat-- ter? The question was not unpleasant, and he bared his soul in response.

"She was a little older than you are. She would go on about being my successor, even as a woman, and she went to a school in America. She was an exceptional daughter…"

Reaching for the memories he had buried so deeply, Isshin began reminiscing to nobody in particular.

It was back when Ikumi was still an employee of Shijima Motors. The committee had been dragging its feet with her pet project.

In her straightforward style, Ikumi had been explaining her self-driving car concept to then-president Isshin and his yes-men—or rather, the men who would plot to drive him from the company. But Isshin, younger than he was now, had cut her off before she could fin- ish and rejected her idea.

"People can only appreciate cars through the act of driving them. Nobody will want a self-driving car!"

"You may be right," Ikumi had said, standing up with the compa- ny's motto behind her: WITH SPIRIT ALONE, WE CAN SOAR. "Maybe that's what cars used to be. But times are changing. It's a natural pro- gression for software to take over driving, even the auto industry as a whole." She made her point levelheadedly yet firmly.

"The day that hardware succumbs to software is the day the auto industry dies!" He impatiently slammed his hands down on the table, and a silence fell over his men.

Some of his men looked disapprovingly at Ikumi, and others made sounds of agreement with Isshin. Exchanging looks, they returned to whispering among themselves.

Ikumi sighed deeply, not bothering to hide her disappointment. "This company has no vision, no plan. Just memories of the distant past and a knack for tripping over its own feet." She gathered the papers in front of her and walked to the exit, her heels clacking. She then looked back up at the company motto that had been at her back moments ago.

WITH SPIRIT ALONE, WE CAN SOAR.

A younger Isshin, a dreamer and an innovator, had surely believed those words at the company's inception.

"…Oh, and, sir? If I were you, I'd change your motto."

With a sunny smile, she left the meeting room. Isshin's desire to call after her was buried under his anger. He had been betrayed by his precious daughter, his most trusted employee.

Back then, I believed she would one day understand how I felt and return to my side. But that day never came. The next letter from Ikumi's residence was to notify me of her death.

Kokone's father had fallen for a woman just like him—somebody who told it like it was.

She must have been such a cool person… Kokone almost broke out in tears, thinking about her mother. *But I can't cry now. He doesn't know who I am; he'll think I'm weird. Maybe if I tell him I'm his granddaughter now, he'll listen to what I have to say?*

While Kokone was debating this internally, he suddenly spoke.

"But I must defeat that demon…"

"Wha—?!"

"…with these two hands."

Kokone turned to Isshin and received quite a shock.

The man sitting next to her was the king of Heartland.

* * *

"When did I fall asleep?"

Kokone panicked. Now that Isshin had finished his story about Ikumi, she needed to tell him that she was his granddaughter and clear Momotarou's name, but she was now taking a nap, apparently.

Though she wasn't aware of it, she was rather annoyed with her special power this time around.

Before she knew it, her surroundings had turned into Heartland. She was still Kokone, not Ancien.

"What'll I do...?"

The king of Heartland slowly stood up and glared at the giant demon rising from the sea. Without so much as a glance at Kokone, he returned to the castle with the soldiers who had come to his aid.

As Kokone watched him blankly, Joy crawled out of her sack. "He's leaving!"

"Is this a dream?" Kokone asked, still unable to process what was happening.

"Yeah, this is the dream world."

"Of course it is... But it doesn't feel like a dream..."

Kokone was wondering what to make of this unusual sense when she heard a nasty voice behind her.

"You had me worried there. I thought you might tell him you were his granddaughter." Bewan appeared from behind a tree.

"Beardy?! Why are you here?!"

"I have a private jet," Bewan boasted.

"It's not even your jet! It's the king's!" Joy retorted with disgust.

"Humph." Bewan scoffed, confident that it would be his soon enough.

"Grandfather didn't know who I was... Why?"

"Your father is unscrupulous, but at least he's honorable. He kept his promise to the king and didn't contact him at all. There's a line between honor and stupidity... Thanks to him, though, the king fully believed our lies." With a menacing smile, Bewan sneered down at Kokone, as if to say that all honorable people were stupid.

Soldiers encircled Kokone, pointing their blades at her, and Kokone realized why this dream felt different from the rest.

"Ancien would beat these soldiers if she fought them, but I can't...?!"

A fear welled up within her that she had never felt as Ancien, and

Kokone understood that though this was a dream, it wasn't actually. Her father's fairy tale about Ancien had already ended.

"Does that mean this is reality?!"

Joy looked dubiously at Kokone, who wasn't fighting. Bewan captured the pair without resistance.

"I'll be taking the magic tablet." Bewan wrested it from Kokone's grip. "Now Heartland is mine!"

Victorious, Bewan smirked. Kokone glared at him in defiance.

Meanwhile, the king of Heartland was watching the demon from above as it climbed up into the Gulf Area. The last Engine Head intercepted it in an effort to prevent it from reaching the factory, but it was no match for the demon's immense strength.

The town was engulfed in explosions and black smoke.

"If only I had believed in the power of magic earlier…" The king of Heartland's regrets echoed through his chamber, heard by none.

* * *

In the reception area of the police station, Morio was waiting with a resistance member for Momotarou to be released. His companion was Tani, the fattest of the three men. According to him, Momotarou had been detained in this police station from the get-go because Watanabe had accused him of theft. So the resistance's leader, the head researcher at Shijima Tech (nicknamed Old Man En), had notified the police that Watanabe's accusations were fraudulent before Morio and the others had gotten here. According to him, the charges against Momotarou would soon be cleared.

"Things went fairly smoothly, which might be because the police didn't trust Watanabe," Tani had said, then contacted his resistance fellows at headquarters and asked them whether Kokone had arrived there.

Morio was worried sick about her after she went to Shijima

Headquarters alone and without much money. Kokone was so clueless sometimes, it was hard to think of her as a modern high schooler. She was fiery, but that also meant she might act recklessly. To top it off, the tablet she had believed was magic was just a regular piece of electronic equipment.

The bespectacled man (named Iwazaki) lent Morio his phone so he could send numerous messages to Kokone's tablet, but she hadn't responded. Unbeknownst to him, Morio had started fidgeting with anxiety.

Tani was speaking with the resistance at headquarters on his phone, and it didn't sound like things were going well. "What?! ... Okay, got it. We'll make preparations on our end, too." Tani hung up, his expression grim. "This is bad. It seems Kokone met the chairman, but she wasn't able to tell him who she was."

"Huh? Why...?"

Kokone had been so determined to clear Momotarou's name, and Morio found it hard to believe she had failed.

"And even worse, Watanabe took her away afterward."

"What?!" Morio exclaimed.

The elevator dinged. The pair looked over and saw that the two interrogating officers were leading the newly freed Momotarou to them.

"Uncle Momo!"

Momotarou had no idea why Morio was there nor why he looked so desperate. "...If it isn't Morio! Why are you here?" he asked bluntly.

Morio impatiently shouted, "It doesn't matter! Kokone's in trouble!"

When he heard that his daughter was in danger, Momotarou's expression immediately darkened.

Momotarou's former comrades brought him up to speed in the station wagon on their way to the Shijima Motors headquarters.

"...I see. They wanted to steal Ikumi's data because the demo vehicle for the Olympics isn't working properly..."

Iwazaki nodded from next to Momotarou. "That's right. But that was Watanabe's plan, and the chairman doesn't know about it."

Momotarou's expression didn't even twitch after hearing that. His past experiences had left him jaded.

"…Still, that's got nothing to do with me."

"But…!" The reply left no room for argument, but Iwazaki still protested. A gloom descended on the resistance's members.

In the driver's seat, Tani gripped the steering wheel and looked over to Old Man En for support.

The silent man finally spoke. "…You're a great man, and you've achieved great things without our help."

Momotarou turned his attention from the window to the other man.

Old Man En continued, as if he had been waiting for the response. "But if you've been keeping the original code to yourself, how is that any different from what Watanabe's doing? Ikumi's magic spell wasn't written for any one person."

Momotarou looked back out the window, swallowing his desire to argue against his former superior. He hadn't mean to hoard it by any means, but upon reflection, maybe it was as Old Man En said.

The resistance, meanwhile, interpreted Momotarou's body language to mean he had taken offense and was doubling down on his stance.

Only Morio understood how Momotarou felt. He knew Momotarou hadn't been keeping the code to himself and had used it to help the people around him, no matter how much the town might ridicule him.

But he couldn't find a way to verbalize the truth, either.

At the same time, a riderless motorcycle followed the station wagon carrying Momotarou and the resistance along the crowded Bayshore Route. That motorcycle was the S-193 Heart that Morio had sent back to Shimotsui from Osaka.

Why Heart had taken that highway, nobody knew.

*   *   *

After they were taken into the castle, Kokone and Joy were forced into the elevator with Bewan and his soldiers. The elevator climbed up and up with no indication of where it might stop.

"So how are you going to take over Heartland?" Kokone asked Bewan, who grinned with confidence.

"Heartland's Engine Heads are now gone. That demon can only be defeated by an Engine Head powered by magic."

"Is that right?" Kokone didn't know the rest of this story, because it had never been told to her. And the events unfolding before her right now were happening in reality. Probably.

The elevator reached its destination, and its doors slowly opened. Bewan ushered her off, and she found herself atop a scaffold overlooking several giant hangars—the Engine Head maintenance plant.

But as Bewan had said, not a single one remained.

"What use is the magic spell if there are no more of them?"

Bewan laughed off Kokone's naive question and wordlessly walked on.

A siren echoed throughout the hangar, and an Engine Head model that was completely new to the fairy tale appeared from deep within.

"This is my secret weapon that will make this nation mine!" crowed Bewan, ecstatic.

Despite its incredibly sleek design, the machine seemed vaguely malevolent to Kokone's eyes.

"It looks evil."

"Nonsense. Look at its lustrous tricolor body! We will launch once the king's Engine Heads are fully destroyed. Then I will shoulder the dejected nation's hopes and become the new king!" Bewan proudly puffed out his chest.

Joy leaped onto him in anger. "You crook! You've been lying to the king this entire time!"

The stuffed animal pummeled Bewan's face with soft fists, but Bewan easily brushed it off and kicked it away.

"I'll do whatever it takes to get the throne."

Kokone cradled the defeated Joy and glared at Bewan. "And you call yourself an adult?!"

"...Hmph." The criticism rolled off Bewan like water off a duck's back, and he laughed. "I have no more use for you. I feared only Ancien, the magic user. You may go."

"Then give me back the tablet!"

"Fine, why not?"

Bewan had already extracted the spell from the tablet and installed it into his Engine Head. He produced the device from his breast pocket, reached out past the handrail, and pretended to drop it.

"No!"

Bewan played with the tablet some more, enjoying Kokone's reactions.

Only the lowest of the low gloated like this. Momotarou had taught Kokone how to deal with such people when she was a child. The worst thing you could do was to indulge them.

Bewan had believed she would beg him to return the tablet. But she, like her father, refused to show weakness and eyed him scornfully.

Irritated, he unintentionally let go of the tablet.

"Ah!"

With Joy in her arms, Kokone overcame her fear and vaulted over the handrail without hesitation.

Bewan was shocked. Nobody would survive a drop from this dizzying height. Before he could stop himself, he was leaning over the handrail to search for Kokone.

"I don't see her...?"

Kokone had landed on a ridge below. The tablet was in her hands—she had snagged it by the corner at the last possible moment.

Bewan instinctively breathed a sigh of relief.

"…T-too close…" Kokone made sure the device was intact, then looked down from her landing spot and began to appreciate how high up she was. *I wonder where I am in real life.* She couldn't let Bewan get away with dropping her mother and father's precious tablet from this height.

Kokone stood up carefully on the twenty-inch-wide ridge. Still carrying Joy, she glared up at Bewan as he leaned over the handrail.

"I can't believe you! …Who raised you, you jerk?!"

Bewan was angry at himself for worrying about Kokone. "Ugh… Obnoxious girl."

I'll get you back somehow…, he thought, but then the elevator's doors opened.

"What is this ruckus?! Bewan, explain yourself!" demanded an imperious voice.

The king of Heartland marched toward them, accompanied by two soldiers.

Bewan was immediately flustered. "Oh! Um, well, I was attempting to capture this suspicious intruder, and…"

Though Bewan was smiling in an attempt to smooth things over, the king of Heartland didn't spare him so much as a glance and instead looked up at the Engine Head in the hangar.

"What is this Engine Head?"

"Yes, this one was made as a precautionary measure…," lied Bewan, wringing his hands. He hoped his hollow explanation would satisfy the king.

But the king betrayed Bewan's hopes and looked over the handrails. "And are they these suspicious intruders you speak of?"

The king looked at Kokone, who smiled awkwardly back at him, unsure of what to say. Joy, however, waved broadly at the king as if they were old friends.

"That plushie…"

Seeing Joy, the king finally recalled the answer to the question he had been struggling with. But he decided he wanted to hear what sort of excuse Bewan planned to make before he said anything.

Glaring at Bewan, the king sternly ordered his soldiers, "Bring those two over here!"

As the soldiers dutifully attempted to climb over the railing, the entire building shook with a loud rumble.

"Aaahh!"

The soldiers had immediately grabbed on to the railing, but Kokone was on a thin ledge without any supports to speak of. She ended up bumping her rear against the wall behind her and pushing herself off.

Huh?! What's happening to me in reality?

Kokone was falling from a height of about five hundred feet, and without Ancien's knack for making quick decisions, she could do little more than flail in midair. She managed to grab on to the railing of a hanging platform used for making repairs, and she dangled from it.

Carrying the tablet, Joy climbed up onto the platform and held a hand out to Kokone.

"Kokone!"

The girl channeled her strength into her quivering arm, trying to pull herself up.

* * *

The car carrying Momotarou, Morio, and the resistance members finally made it to Shijima Motors' headquarters. But when they got out, they found a large crowd in front of the entrance, so big that they couldn't get in. Among them were television reporters, camera operators, and other people from the mainstream media. The clearly distressed security guards were struggling to keep them at bay.

What was happening? Momotarou grabbed a man at the back of the crowd.

"Hey, what's all this about?"

The man turned around, his expression serious.

"Well, I don't really understand it myself, but apparently, a girl is in huge trouble on the thirtieth floor," he explained at length.

A girl... Momotarou and Morio shared a glance.

"You think...?"

"Kokone?"

They looked up at the building, but they could see nothing of what might be happening inside. Momotarou barged through the crowd in front of him toward the lobby.

"Hey, let us through!"

Morio chased after him, not wanting to be left behind.

"Let us through!"

The resistance members weren't far behind.

Following their lead, the media and onlookers started pushing forward, too.

"Get out of here—you can wait!" shouted Momotarou, forcing his way through the entrance.

"Uncle Momo!"

As Morio was swept toward the back of the crowd, Momotarou grabbed his hand and yanked the doors open.

*   *   *

"What the hell is this?!" Momotarou exclaimed.

Momotarou had barged through the mob and entered the lobby of the Shijima Headquarters—or so he had thought. But the space where the lobby should have been was a dimly lit hangar of some kind, at least 650 feet high. A giant mechanical scaffold stretched nearly to the ceiling.

Startled, Momotarou looked back at the entrance he had just come through, but the lobby's glass front had been replaced by giant metal doors nearly as high as the room itself, and a giant black demon was trying to tear them open.

For a moment, Momotarou was speechless. He looked down and saw that his own dress shirt and slacks had been replaced by a pair of parachute pants and a sleeveless track jacket with a skull on the back. Panicked, he whirled toward Morio, who was still wearing the same T-shirt and pants as before.

"What's going on?" Momotarou asked.

Morio had noticed the changes, too. "Is Kokone asleep again?!"

Morio was convinced this was the same phenomenon that had occurred the last time Kokone went to sleep, and he explained the previous night's events to Momotarou.

"So this is how Kokone imagined Peach?" Momotarou gave himself another once-over.

Four little people rushed to join them. When he took a closer look, he realized they were identical to the resistance members.

"To be fair, the little people in the fairy tale were based off these guys," said Momotarou.

The four looked uncertainly up at Momotarou.

Behind them, the giant demon was still shaking the front gate, attempting to pry it open. The building shook incessantly under its strength.

Momotarou looked up at the scaffold as though he had suddenly remembered something. He saw Kokone above, clinging to a suspended platform for her life.

"Kokone!"

But with her attention focused entirely on gripping the platform, she couldn't hear Momotarou's voice.

"Uncle Momo, at this rate…"

"I know. We'll need to get creative to save her."

Momotarou was already running through the rules of the fairy-tale world—he had created it, after all.

"Let's activate the Engine Head, Morio! Give me that!"

Momotarou grabbed Morio's bag and slung it over his own shoulder. The AR goggles were inside. With those, they should be able to operate the Engine Head.

The little people of the resistance broke out in smiles at Momotarou's exclamation. Finally, Peach—no, Momotarou—would use the original code!

"…Don't get me wrong. I just want to save Kokone," he said to hide his embarrassment, then started racing up the scaffold toward Bewan's Engine Head.

Kokone felt her grip loosening on the railing as the platform shook incessantly. Joy struggled, too, trying to pull her up, but the plushie's arms were not very strong.

"Save that girl!"

In response to their liege's order, the soldiers securely tied a length of rope to the railing of the scaffold and started rappelling down toward her.

My schemes will be discovered if they save that girl, Bewan thought. He needed to pull the king of Heartland away.

"The demon is right there! You needn't concern yourself with such plebeians. Please, my lord, you must escape."

The king glared at Bewan and his false smile, and he issued an order to his soldiers.

"Arrest that man!"

Stunned, Bewan found himself surrounded. In a pained voice, he began, "My lord, I was—"

"You idiot! Do you think you can continue fooling me?!" His

expression severe, the king of Heartland looked past the railing, where Joy was still desperately holding on to Kokone.

"I bought that plushie for Ikumi."

Ikumi had always taken good care of it, ever since she was a child. And the girl who had it now…

Only one possibility came to the king's mind. The girl had to be Ikumi's child.

"How many lies have you told me over these years?!"

Realizing that his liege would no longer believe his lies, Bewan grinned widely and allowed his disdain to reveal itself.

"Your Majesty, your plans have failed. Now, let's not have any trouble, and hand me the crown!"

But Bewan's ruse crumbled before the king's overwhelming grandeur.

"I'll listen to what you have to say if we manage to save the kingdom from the demon. Take him away!"

But at that moment, a crash resounded through Heartland Castle's hangar as the demon smashed through the gates.

Momotarou ran up the seemingly eternal spiral staircase as if his life depended on it. His heart was close to bursting by the time he made it to the top of the thirty-story staircase. But there was no time to take a breather—he leaned out over the railing to look for Kokone.

She was still hanging from the same spot on the platform.

"Attagirl! I'll be right there!" Momotarou turned toward the Engine Head. There were about twenty-two yards between the scaffold and its entrance. Not a distance you could normally jump. Was there anything he could use to get there? Momotarou scanned the area and saw, at the edge of the scaffolding, a half-extended crane for hauling up building materials. Momotarou vaulted over the handrail without hesitation and sprinted along the top of the crane as fast as he could go. But there were eleven yards between the end of the crane and the Engine Head.

"With spirit alone, we can soar!" shouted Momotarou, then he leaped off the end of the crane.

The wall of air impeded his flight, and everything went into slow motion.

"Almost!"

Momotarou pointed his toes and reached as far as he could toward the ladder on the outside of the Engine Head. The tips of his boots made contact—but his outstretched right hand missed by a hair. Unable to support his weight, his toes slipped off the ladder, and Momotarou plunged toward the ground.

But he couldn't afford to fall here. Momotarou desperately extended his arm and caught the ladder's bottom rung in his right hand. He immediately grabbed on with his left, too, then started racing up the ladder.

Kokone couldn't hold on anymore.

Her right hand began slipping off the platform. Joy was holding her left but didn't have the strength to pull her up.

The king of Heartland could do nothing but watch the two from the scaffolding above, and he was becoming increasingly frustrated.

The demon, having destroyed the gate, was proceeding deeper into the castle. Lava spilled from the cracks in its surface, which appeared and sealed themselves at random, and a blood-curdling howl sounded from its mouth.

The soldiers, motionless with fear, had been unable to get any closer to the platform.

Time was running out.

I won't die here..., thought Kokone, but her grip had finally reached its breaking point, and she fell through the air with a scream. She saw Joy jump from the platform with the tablet.

"No, Joy, don't!"

Suddenly, Kokone was awash in a feeling she had felt only once before, at Washuzan Highland Amusement Park when she was a child. The sensation of floating, like the one she had on attractions that simulated flying.

Is this how dying feels? But when Kokone opened her eyes, she and Joy were being lifted up in an Engine Head's right hand.

"Whoa!" Kokone cheered, looking up at the machine that had looked so evil to her earlier.

However, they weren't out of the woods yet. The demon had noticed the Engine Head and was now reaching for it with its enormous arm. The creature's body was made out of a lava-like substance, and they would be incinerated if it caught them.

But the Engine Head grabbed the demon's arm with its left hand and, shielding Kokone in its other hand, delivered a lunge kick to the demon. The demon's enormous body was launched away and out of the castle, skidding across the ground with a rumble.

This was the power of an Engine Head fueled by magic. Its fluidity and strength were a cut above those before it.

After being literally kicked out of the castle, the monster rolled along the Engine Head–use road that stretched from the castle to the Gulf Area, kicking up a cloud of dust along the way. The people of the town, who were on their way to work, got out of their cars to see what the source of the thunderous sounds and tremors was.

Hot in pursuit, the Engine Head calmly showed itself. It stopped once in front of Heartland Castle and, kneeling down, dropped Kokone off there from the palm of its hand. The palm alone was thirteen feet thick.

Kokone realized the Engine Head she had expected to be a villain had saved her and was now gently lowering her to the ground.

"Is this Engine Head…?"

Kokone hopped off the giant machine's palm. It started off again, and she superimposed her father's image over its gallant figure. It looked about as tall as the Great Seto Bridge.

The Engine Head's cockpit was oddly designed. It consisted of a single pole standing in a bottomless pit, and atop it was a bicycle-shaped instrument that controlled the machine. Momotarou, the AR goggles on his face, was pedaling to control the machine all by himself.

"Kokone… I'm sorry for putting you in danger."

Though his words were not heard, her father was always thinking of his daughter, and she never took her eyes off him.

Momotarou charged the Engine Head toward the shakily recovering demon like a sumo wrestler charging his adversary.

"Graaaah!"

Momotarou pedaled with all his might. The Engine Head's left arm lifted the demon by the hip, then threw it clumsily against the ground. Buildings crumbled in an explosion of dust.

The Engine Head seemed to be winning handily, but Momotarou's stamina was nearly exhausted. The machine would ordinarily operate on magic, and so Momotarou's pedaling would be supplementary. But Bewan had not known that the magic program needed a password and a reboot. So, despite the spell, Momotarou had no choice but to operate the Engine Head manually.

The password entry prompt still blinked on his head-mounted display. The system remained locked.

"Damn it, we need to access the magic…"

"Who's piloting that?" the king of Heartland asked as he watched the spectacle. But nobody there could answer him.

"Wow!" exclaimed Morio, who had joined Kokone.

"Morio! Dad's on that, right?"

"Yeah!" Morio said with both pride and exhilaration. "Uncle Momo's crazy strong!"

The Engine Head punched the demon once more. As the monster staggered, the soldiers in the hangar cheered.

His thunder stolen, Bewan watched the fight without any enthusiasm at first, but then he noticed that the soldiers were distracted, and he gave a sinister smile. He shook his handcuffed arms and produced a magic phone from his sleeve.

"…That's my Engine Head. This kingdom belongs to me!"

In his frustration, Bewan had finally decided to use forbidden magic. His face twitching, he tapped the screen with only his fingertips.

The soldiers, noticing the unusual activity, turned around.

"Hey, you!"

"Huh?! He's using a curse!"

Bewan raised his phone above his head, as if to declare that it was too late. The spell's text was already on its screen.

"Shijima Motors' self-driving car was not completed before the Olympics. For proof, go to the following URL: http://www?????"

Bewan, prepared to set Heartland ablaze now that he had determined it would never be his, tapped the ENTER key with a malicious fingertip.

With an unpleasant noise upon its sending, the curse resonated with the glass tubing on the typewriter in Bewan's room. The spell glowed eerily within it, blew open the lid, and spread throughout Heartland.

The demon screamed in agony but, once again, stood back up. Momotarou threw a full-bodied punch at it. The creature's upper body snapped backward under the blow, and it crumpled to its knees.

"Have I done it?" Momotarou said, envisioning victory but heaving with effort.

Kokone, Morio, and the four little resistance members cheered from the castle.

But the demon's death cries were only the beginning. Using Bewan's curse, the scattered fragments recombined themselves into the form of a bat, and just as Kokone and the others noticed the dark cloud swirling around the bat, the mist immediately blanketed the area around the castle. Consumed by the cloud, the town began bursting into flames, and the smoke combined with the darkness, plunging the town into a deeper black.

The Engine Head, too, was spontaneously combusting.

"What's happening?"

Heartland was engulfed in flames.

Kokone could do nothing but watch the enormous machine, without a clue what was happening.

"Burn, burn! Everything that doesn't go my way should burn!" Bewan continued to curse Heartland, even after multiple soldiers struck the phone from his hands and wrestled him to the ground. Bewan's spell spread, becoming not only his hatred, but the animosity of others, consuming Heartland.

"You...!" Even the majestic king of Heartland could do nothing but glare at Bewan.

Kokone had started running toward the burning, motionless Engine Head. Not that she could do anything without magic, but she couldn't sit still and watch Momotarou fight by himself. Morio and the little people felt the same, chasing after Kokone.

But a swarm of black bats appeared to block their way and attacked them.

"Pguh!"

"Waaah!"

Desperately swatting at the horde, none of them could make any progress. The thing that was once a demon had shaped itself into something vaguely resembling a swarm of bats. One portion of the swarm re-formed itself into a giant tentacle and shot into the air, then changed into lava and covered the Engine Head.

"Dad!" Kokone dashed through the burning town toward the mechanical giant.

"Kokone!" Morio, ignoring the bats, chased after her.

"Ha-ha-ha-ha-ha!"

Losing his grip on his sanity, Bewan cackled maniacally at the sight of the burning town. His kowtowing, empty words, and expensive planning throughout all those years had been for a singular purpose: to seize the throne. But that was now over and done. Bewan lost his mind and howled.

"Let it all burn!" he hollered.

The cry reached the cursed swarm of bats, which flew over to Bewan and engulfed him in fire.

"This message is from Shijima Headquarters' IP."

"Some employee named Watanabe wrote it. (LOL)"

"For fame? An internal struggle? A marketing tactic?"

Bewan's magic phone displayed a stream of new curses, and it, too, was swallowed by the flames.

The soldiers who had been Bewan's captors could do nothing but watch the rapid turn of events.

"Aaaaaagh!" Bewan let out a deathly scream. He became part of the swarm of bats and flew away, leaving behind only his crazed laughter.

The king observed the whole scene with an expression full of pity. He then started toward the Engine Head's pilot, the only person who was still fighting to protect the nation. The king contemplated while he walked.

I cornered Bewan, so I must be the one to deal with the consequences of his actions.

The newly revived demon transformed into something resembling candy and wrapped itself around the Engine Head, which was now immobile after its systems had gone up in flames. The machine lost its footing and started to fall. Momotarou, still in the cockpit, was nearly thrown from his saddle by the shock. He barely managed to hold on to the grip and avoided falling.

But before he knew it, the bats had infiltrated the cockpit and were attacking him.

The password entry prompt was still blinking on Momotarou's AR display.

"So we really can't beat that thing without magic…" Momotarou searched his pockets for his phone. "Kokone… The magic spell!"

The spell would activate if the password were typed into the tablet. Just as he took his phone out to tell Kokone this crucial fact, the Engine Head tilted even farther.

"Gah…!"

The phone slipped from Momotarou's palm and dropped down the pit, out of sight.

He had no way of telling Kokone what to do.

Momotarou took the AR goggles off, gritted his teeth, and began pedaling once more—but his stamina was nearly gone.

"Daaaad!" shouted Kokone, standing at the tip of a shattered section of highway the demon had destroyed on its rampage.

But the Engine Head continued to burn, with no signs of moving.

The town around them had become a pile of rubble, burning in a cloud of black smoke. It was an overwhelmingly depressing sight.

"…What can I do…?!" In her panic, Kokone was beginning to lose sight of her objective.

"Kokone!" yelled Joy, breaking its silence. Still clutching Kokone's shoulder, it pointed at the tablet in Kokone's hand.

"We can power the Engine Head using magic, Kokone!"

"Oh, right…!" She realized she could write the rest of the fairy tale herself. She lifted the tablet over her head with both arms and typed the spell.

"With spirit alone, we can soar. Engine Head, fulfill Mom and Dad's dreams and save Heartland!" Kokone declared, then stretched her pointer finger toward the screen. "Enter!"

A colorless light suddenly shone within the cockpit where Momotarou was feebly pedaling. Momotarou knew what it was—the light of magic. Soon, it had enveloped the entire Engine Head.

The machine regained its strength and tore the lava around it apart. The light shone from its every inch, racing through Heartland, extinguishing every flame, and blowing away all the smoke. Even the cloud of dust suspended over Heartland was erased, and the sky was restored to its blue glory.

After the brilliant light scattered the bats, they regrouped at one point—they meant to torch Heartland and the Engine Head one last time before they lost their strength.

Momotarou gave the magic-powered machine its last order, entrusting it with his final wish.

"Fly, Engine Head."

The machine sprouted wings, and the booster rockets in its legs ignited. Its booming footsteps and the sound of its liftoff resounded through Heartland Castle, and the Engine Head rose slowly into the blue sky.

The swarm of bats ascended after it.

Kokone and Morio shielded themselves from the blast of the rocket engines. The few flames still burning throughout the town were blown out.

"Whoaaa!"

The Engine Head accelerated its ascent, and the black swarm of bats followed it.

Kokone watched over her mother and father's dream from the ground, dust swirling around her.

*   *   *

"Guh…!" Momotarou, alone, endured g-forces he had never before encountered.

The Engine Head rocketed straight into the sky, through the clouds, through the stratosphere, and right as it was about to enter low earth orbit, it was mobbed by the swarm of bats.

But that had been Momotarou's aim.

"I wonder if the king'll acknowledge Ikumi's magic now."

Momotarou prayed in the zero-gravity cockpit that Ikumi's labor would put out Heartland's flames once and for all.

Eventually, the Engine Head's shining blue wings dissolved, and the machine floated along in orbit in a ball of pitch-blackness.

Kokone and Morio saw a singular black speck in the blue sky where the Engine Head had flown.

"…Hmm? Something's wrong." Morio's eyes widened in realization. "Maybe Uncle Momo can't come back on his own?"

"Oh no! What do we do? We need to save Dad!"

"But…!"

All they had was the tablet, and now that they'd used Ikumi's magic, there was nothing left in it.

Their palms broke out in anxious sweat. Then they heard a familiar engine sound from behind them.

"Huh?!"

The two turned around together and saw the S-193 heading toward them, kicking up dust behind it. The motorcycle drifted to a halt in front of them, then quickly transformed into the humanoid Heart, as if to apologize for making them wait.

"Heart?! Why are you here?" Kokone asked, her voice raised in shock.

Morio cocked his head, unsatisfied. "Why? I thought I ordered it to go home…" He had intended for it to head back to Shimotsui when he had activated the autopilot at the gasoline stand in Osaka.

"Thanks, Morio!" Kokone said, thinking Morio had called Heart here. She then leaped up onto its back.

With Kokone astride, Heart began running to lift off but could not muster enough speed.

"Aaaahh!" Kokone screamed as they fell toward the sea, but then the engine revved, and like the Engine Head, Heart sprouted wings and flew up, high into the sky.

Heart ascended straight toward the Engine Head. Clinging to its back, Kokone couldn't even open her eyes.

Eventually, the atmospheric pressure decreased, and the air thinned.

"This could be bad…," said Kokone.

Just then, the Engine Head came into view as a ball of pure darkness. Heart plunged through the wall of bats, circled halfway around the Engine Head, and flung Kokone into the zero-gravity space. Using that momentum, Kokone floated toward the Engine Head's main hatch. She grabbed the knob and yanked with all her might.

"I'm here to save you, Dad."

But the hatch would not open, and she was slowly running out of oxygen.

*   *   *

Kokone suddenly returned to consciousness, sensing that her body was floating. She opened her eyes, fearing she might have torn off the handle.

"…Huh?"

Was she falling, not floating?

She had been in space not moments ago, and yet she was now tumbling in slow motion through the Shijima Headquarters' lobby. She looked down fearfully, and past the banners and the balloons, she saw people the size of ants walking around far below her.

"?!"

As Kokone fully awoke, the slow-motion fall turned to regular speed.

"H-huh? Whaaaa—?"

Then somebody grabbed Kokone's arm.

"Guh!"

Kokone looked to see who had snagged her arm and saved her from her fall. It was Momotarou in a dress shirt, a rare sight for her.

"? ...I thought I was saving Dad! Why's he saving me?"

Kokone hadn't fully recovered from her dream. Momotarou, in contrast, was sweating bullets, grinding his teeth.

Apparently, she and Momotarou were hanging from the metal portion of the trusses of the building's glass ceiling. Chairman Shijima on the thirtieth floor, the media pouring through the lobby's entrance, Shijima's many employees on various floors, and Morio and the resistance in the lobby—all watched with bated breath as Momotarou hung from the structure, clinging to Kokone's arm.

"Dad, I think I fell asleep during something really important. Did I do something I shouldn't have?"

Terrified, Kokone imagined the disaster from her dream in real life.

"Did I make trouble for you, Dad?"

"I dunno. We were like this when I came to."

Kokone wondered whether Momotarou had told her that to calm her worries, but in truth, he had no recollection of what had actually happened, either. Momotarou had been trying to save Kokone and Heartland from disaster.

He forced a smile, hoping to give Kokone some peace of mind.

But she watched him uneasily. Momotarou smiled like that only when things weren't looking good.

Watching her expression, Momotarou saw Ikumi's face as she had dangled from the Engine Head's deck.

He couldn't let that happen again. He channeled all his strength into his right hand, but his palm became sweaty and lost its grip. Kokone slid down, suspended only by her wrist.

The two closed their eyes.

"I'll come back whenever you need me. Take care of Kokone until then."

Ikumi's voice.

Craaash! The S-193 Heart smashed through a large glass window on the first floor, spraying shards everywhere.

"Why is Heart here?!" Morio couldn't hide his shock.

Heart wrapped the wire connected to the giant balloon around its body and drove itself through the mass of people.

Soon, the enormous Shijima mascot balloon floated down, right above Morio's head.

As if to say *Use this*, Heart stopped in front of Morio, its back wheel still spinning.

"I see!" Morio's eyes widened. He looked up and checked where Kokone was, then took the end of the wire wrapped around Heart.

Hearing Ikumi's voice, Momotarou looked down, and Heart came flying into view. Heart was trying to save them at great cost to itself. The giant balloon slowly floated its way to below Kokone. It would be under her soon.

But his arm couldn't hold on any longer.

"Fly, Kokone!" Momotarou yelled, then fell with Kokone toward the balloon. He hugged her body to his in midair and plummeted through the many banners in an attempt to slow their descent by even the slightest bit. But the speed was still unsafe.

Heart, now free of the wires, suddenly accelerated and used the collapsing banners as ramps to ride upward.

"Heart!"

The balloon was still a bit shy of the falling pair; Morio thought he saw Heart transform into its humanoid form and push it the rest of the way.

The balloon moved under Kokone and Momotarou, and they landed on its back. A hole opened from the impact, and the inflatable loudly and slowly deflated as it descended over the mass media and merely curious. The customers fled.

Morio and the resistance members ran to assist Kokone and Momotarou, who were swallowed by the balloon where it had landed. Now on the floor, the mascot leaked air and slowly come to rest flat.

As the many onlookers held their breath, a motorcycle, damaged from the impact, and Kokone, collapsed inside the sidecar with only her leg poking out, emerged from the balloon's fabric.

"Kokone?!" Morio called out worriedly.

As she rubbed her head, Kokone's face appeared from the sidecar.

"…Yeah!!" Morio's triumphant cry was the first in a roar of cheers. He tried to run over to Kokone's side, but he was deflected by the media and quickly swallowed by the wave of people.

"Hey, what just happened?!"

"Camera guy, get over here!"

"Why were you up so high?"

"Do you know anything about this e-mail?"

Cameras flashed all around Kokone, and a continuous stream of microphones and cameras were thrust at her. Kokone, not quite sure what was happening, cocked her head and searched for familiar faces. Despite this, the reporters continued to pummel her with questions.

"Do you have something to do with the recent events at Shijima Motors?"

"Kokone!" a familiar voice called from within the swarm of reporters. Morio appeared, clawing through the crowd.

Kokone's expression brightened. "Morio!"

Morio extended his hand, and Kokone stood up from the sidecar with his help. The media surrounding them doubled, and cameras flashed. A few regular bystanders took pictures with their phones, too.

Without thinking, Kokone leaped into Morio's arms.

"What's happening?"

"I'd like to know!"

The journalists hovering around the two as they looked at each other suddenly went silent and parted to clear a path. The chairman of Shijima Motors, the regal and stern-looking Isshin Shijima, had arrived.

Isshin slowly advanced toward the two. The media and employees there simply stood up straighter, the heavy atmosphere preventing them from doing anything else. Some of the reporters had come here on the word that a Shijima employee had texted "*The self-driving car that Shijima Motors was meant to debut at the Olympics is not yet complete*," but not even they could jab a microphone out at the chairman.

Isshin looked at the sidecar Kokone had been riding in. That motorcycle was the first vehicle Shijima Motors had ever produced, and with his own two eyes, he had seen that old model drive itself as if by magic and save Kokone. Perplexed, Isshin muttered to Kokone as if speaking to himself:

"You completed the self-driving car."

Isshin then gave Kokone another once-over. At the sight of the plushie she was holding so tightly, the one he had gifted Ikumi, Isshin recognized some of his daughter in the young girl.

"You're…"

Kokone smiled at the speechless chairman. "My name is Kokone Morikawa. It's written with the characters for 'heart' and 'wing'!"

"…!"

Isshin finally understood what Ikumi had meant in telling him she would change the company motto.

"When our hearts have wings, we can soar freely through the skies."

Ikumi had wanted to change Shijima's spirit—and she had imbued this girl with that dream.

Isshin slowly closed his eyes and smiled, thinking of Ikumi.

Kokone realized he knew her to be Ikumi and Momotarou's child.

Now's my chance to clear Dad's name! she thought.

The reporters started up again, wanting to know what the fallen girl and Chairman Shijima's relation was. Kokone searched for her father in the crowd.

Momotarou, who had crawled out from under the balloon's fabric and now hid within the mass of people, considered sneaking out unnoticed by the media. But concerned about how Kokone was doing, he took a peek at her between the people. There he saw Isshin Shijima, the man he had meant to speak to but had not even seen for eighteen years.

"What do you mean, you've perfected the self-driving car?"

Kokone finally found Momotarou amid the flurry of tactless questions directed at her and Isshin. Isshin followed her gaze and saw him as well. She handed the tablet to Morio and walked toward Momotarou, took his hand, and led him to Isshin. She then took Isshin's hand in her other hand.

The media and the curious onlookers had no idea what was occurring but took photos of the "Handshake That Would Go Down in History." They told the world that Shijima's self-driving automobile was complete, and better than expected.

"The Olympics are always rife with drama. To end the seventeen-day tournament, the athletes of the world were driven into the closing ceremonies by a procession of self-driving automobiles created through the combined efforts of multiple automobile manufacturers led by Shijima Motors."

The news relayed the events of the Tokyo Olympics closing ceremony, which had only just ended.

"The fully autonomous automobile was in production until just before the ceremony, and many warned of potential dangers, but there were no notable accidents, and the athletes, as well as the media, have reacted positively to its innovations…"

A freshly lit incense stick stood in front of Ikumi's altar, a single wisp of white smoke rising from its tip, and with it the scent of *Obon*. The figure made of cucumber had been replaced by one made of eggplant a day ago.

Kokone called out to Momotarou, who was lighting a welcoming fire by himself in the backyard.

"Hey, why did you change the altar's cucumber to an eggplant?"

Momotarou raised his face and looked at Kokone as she walked over carrying a watermelon. She was wearing a *yukata*, a traditional Japanese garment, the first she had ever put on by herself. It looked good on her.

"Cucumbers are like horses, and eggplants are like cows. Cows are slow, and I thought it'd be better since I don't want Mom going away too quickly once she gets here." He stood up and stretched his back.

"Oh, so that's what that means."

"I don't really know, either." Momotarou smiled to hide his embarrassment and looked up at the sky. Tall, fluffy clouds gleamed white in the blue expanse. "What happened to Morio?"

"He said there's a seminar at his university, so he had to leave yesterday."

"Oh, really."

The sliding door to the altar room opened, and through it walked

Isshin, also wearing a *yukata*. He had come to stay at their house in Okayama upon completing his work at the Olympics.

"That *yukata* looks good on you," said Kokone.

"You think so?" Isshin broke into a smile at his granddaughter's compliment.

With Kokone in the middle, the three sat side by side on the porch—but there was still some awkwardness.

"…So what do you plan to do?" Isshin asked Momotarou.

Momotarou had handed over Ikumi's program and the data from the self-driving cars he had completed in Okayama to Shijima so that the company could complete their self-driving car in time for the opening ceremony. It had gone swimmingly only because of that and the resistance's concerted efforts.

After they'd witnessed Ikumi's dream come true together, any unpleasantness between Isshin and Momotarou had dissipated. The chairman had offered Momotarou a position as a technician at Shijima Motors.

Momotarou unwrapped the towel he always wore from his head, slicked his hair back, and answered Isshin's query. "I think each person has a place that's right for them. I think mine is here, working day by day."

"I see…" Isshin, though disappointed, had expected as much. "Summer vacation will be over after *Obon*. What'll you do, Kokone? Do you want to prepare for exams in Tokyo?" Isshin had expressed that he would like for her to come, if she so wished.

"Hmm… I do sort of want to…" Kokone glanced at Momotarou.

Momotarou saw this and faintly smiled, still facing forward. "I don't mind."

Kokone smiled as well. "Then I'll go from time to time, once I figure out where I want to go to college. I want to know more about Mom, too." She looked at her grandfather and father in turn, then smiled again. "Take good care of me, Grandpa, Dad!"

Kokone reminisced on her adventures, though they were only two days ago. She had gone to a land she had never visited; been touched by the sentiments of her father, her mother, and the grandfather she had never known; and learned of all the hopes and dreams that had belonged to her family before she had been born and had grown up here.

Her new life had begun this summer vacation, and she felt refreshed.

Flip to the back for a whole
new look at the world of Heartland.

The first volume of the manga available now!

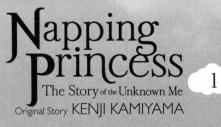

Napping Princess
The Story of the Unknown Me

1

Original Story KENJI KAMIYAMA

Art HANA ICHIKA

Translation: Leighann Harvey · Lettering: Bianca Pistillo

Napping Princess "The Story of the Unknown Me," Volume 1
©Hana ICHIKA 2017
©Kenji Kamiyama/2017 "ANCIEN AND THE MAGIC TABLET" Film Partners
First published in Japan in 2017 by KADOKAWA CORPORATION, Tokyo. English translation rights arranged with KADOKAWA CORPORATION, Tokyo, through TUTTLE-MORI AGENCY, INC., Tokyo.

English translation © 2017 by Yen Press, LLC

Yen Press
1290 Avenue of the Americas
New York, NY 10104

Visit us at yenpress.com
facebook.com/yenpress
twitter.com/yenpress
yenpress.tumblr.com
instagram.com/yenpress

First Yen Press Print Edition: April 2018
The chapters in this volume were originally published as eBooks by Yen Press.

Yen Press is an imprint of Yen Press, LLC.
The Yen Press name and logo are trademarks of Yen Press, LLC.

ISBNs: 978-1-9753-2607-4 (paperback)
978-1-9753-2605-0 (ebook)

Printed in the United States of America

28

GASA
(RUSTLE)

2020年

THIS ISN'T...

...WHAT MIYAKE-SAN PAID YOU FOR THE REPAIRS, IS IT?

DAD!

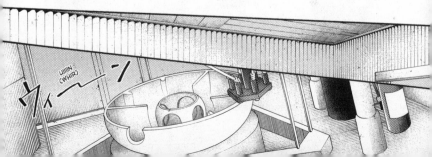

UIIIN
(WHIR)

GU
(GRAB)

BA
(FWIP)

BATA BATA
(THUD)

I-I'M GONNA BE LATE—!!!

THERE.

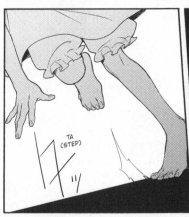
TA
(STEP)

GUGU
(STRAIN)

GI
(CREAK)

GI

GI

TA TA TA TA

OH! THE MAGIC TABLET!

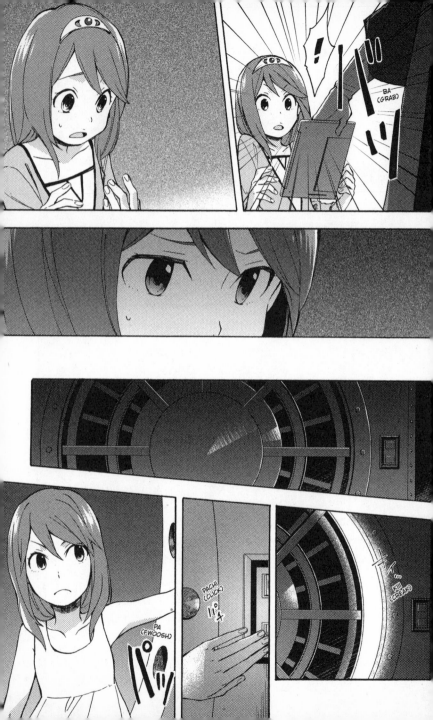

THEN, WHEN SHE WAS SIX, SHE CAST MAGIC ON ALL THE MACHINES IN THE CITY TO MAKE THEM MOVE ON THEIR OWN.

WHOA!

UIIIN (WHIRR)

PI
(BEEP)

ピ

ピ

ピ

JOY

Joy will start moving and talking

POSU
(PLOP)

ぽす

WHEN
SHE
TURNED
THREE,
ANCIEN
USED
MAGIC...

PYON
(HOP)

ピョン

ピョン

PYON

PIKU
(TWITCH)

ピクッ

ENTER!

PLEASED
TO MEET
YOU!

...TO
MAKE THE
STUFFED
ANIMAL THE
KING GAVE
HER, WHO
SHE NAMED

ぷこっ

PEKO
(BOW)

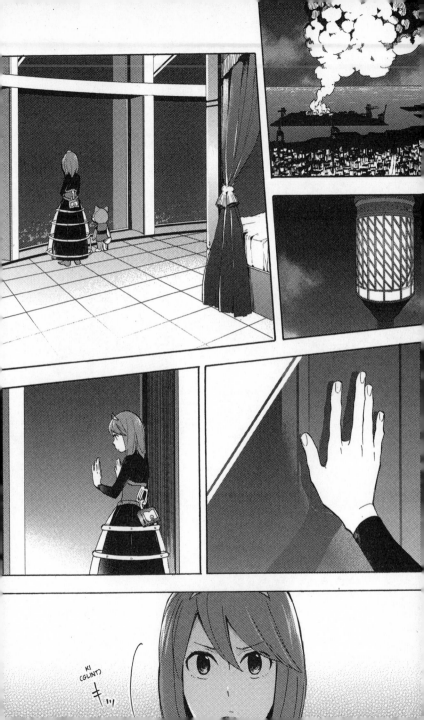

KI
(GLINT)

DESPITE ALL OF THAT, KING HEARTLAND HAD ONE BIG PROBLEM WEIGHING ON HIM...

...AND THAT WOULD BE THAT HIS DEAR DAUGHTER, ANCIEN...

...WAS BORN A MAGIC USER, ONE WHO WOULD BRING TERRIBLE CALAMITY DOWN ON THE KINGDOM.

YOU CAN'T JUST IGNORE THE RULES.

YEAH, I GUESS.

BUT I'M PRETTY ATTACHED TO THIS CAR. I LIKE IT.

THIS IS EVERYDAY LIFE IN EAST-OPOLIS, THE CAPITAL OF HEART-LAND.

IT DOESN'T MATTER HOW CROWDED THE ROADS ARE, OR HOW MUCH YOU LOVE YOUR OLD JALOPY ...

...HAVING EVERYTHING REVOLVE AROUND THE KING'S DECISIONS IS JUST HOW IT'S DONE IN HEARTLAND.

BISHI (JAB)

GET YOURSELF A NEW CAR!

HOW LONG ARE YOU GOING TO KEEP RIDING THIS BIKE?

SFX: TSUKA (STRIDE) TSUKA TSUKA

!

TSUKA TSUKA

IF YOU BREAK THE RULES, IT COMES OUT OF YOUR PAY, YOU KNOW!

GASA (RUSTLE)

AHH!

BA (WHAT?)

HUH?

NO WAY.

HIRA (FLUTTER)

YOU NEED TO GET A NEW CAR TOO.

UGH!

7

GAYA
(CHATTER)
ガヤ

GAYA
ガヤ

I ONLY GOT TO WORK FOUR HOURS TODAY.

...

HERE.

YOU WERE LATE, SO I TOOK SOME OUT.

DAILY WAGE
日当

REALLY ...?

ZA
(STEP)

6

HE
BELIEVE
MACHINE
COULD
BRING
HAPPINES
TO ALL.

FOR THAT
REASON,
MOST
PEOPLE HAVE
TO LEAVE
THE HOUSE
AT FIVE A.M.
TO COME TO
WORK, BUT
THEY STILL
RUN LATE
DUE TO THE
TRAFFIC.

.....

THE
PEOPLE
COME TO THE
CASTLE TO
WORK ON THE
AUTOMOBILE
ASSEMBLY
LINE INSIDE...

...AND AT
FIVE P.M.,
THE NIGHT
WORKERS
COME IN
TO START
THEIR
SHIFTS.

5

GAAA GYROOOD

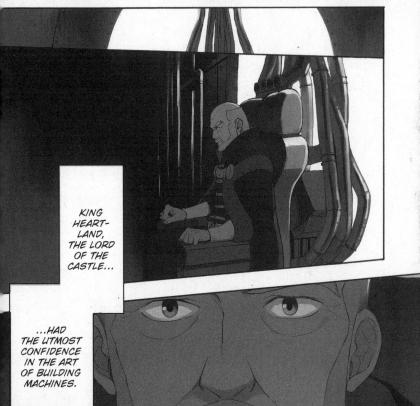

KING HEART-LAND, THE LORD OF THE CASTLE...

...HAD THE UTMOST CONFIDENCE IN THE ART OF BUILDING MACHINES.

THEY WORK AROUND THE CLOCK MAKING MACHINES.

Napping Princess

The Story of the Unknown Me

Original Story: KENJI KAMIYAMA
Art: HANA ICHIKA

ONCE UPON A TIME, THERE WAS A KINGDOM CALLED HEARTLAND WHOSE PEOPLE WERE ALL OBSESSED WITH MAKING MACHINERY.

WHERE'S EVERYONE GOING?

THEY'RE COMING HERE— TO THE HEARTLAND CASTLE.

HYOI (LIFT)
ヒョイ

THE TRAFFIC JAMME AGAIN TODAY.